3

Dear Diary,

Well, I finally made it to my uncle's ranch, and can you believe I was almost run off by my so-called partner, J. D. Pruitt? Seems he's got some strange idea that a pregnant woman has no place on a ranch. But this ranch is the place where I want to raise my child, and no long, lean cowboy with a smile that spells trouble is going to tell me otherwise. Now, if I could just keep my hormones under control every time I see him, I might make a fine cowgirl. And who knows, maybe I'll even rope myself a cowboy daddy for my kid....

Till tomorrow,

Kate

Dear Reader,

I don't know where you live; it could be a nice, warm, *snowless* place. Southern California, maybe, or Florida. Or Hawaii. But as for me, I live right in the snow belt: Connecticut. And I grew up in an even worse spot, weatherwise: western New York state. So I know what blizzards are, because I've had to cope with quite a few in my time. In fact, just a few years ago, we got so many snowstorms—and I had to shovel the driveway so many times—that I joked to all my friends about how I was going steady with my snow shovel. I figured he was the strong, silent type, and he got me out of the house on a regular basis. However, given the opportunity, I would have been happy to trade him in for Randall Watson, the hero of Maris Soule's *The Bachelor, the Beauty and the Blizzard.* If you read the book, I think you'll see why.

While you're in a reading mood, be sure to pick up Mary Starleigh's *The Texan and the Pregnant Cowgirl.* This brand-new author is someone to watch, because she not only has talent, she also has a great sense of humor. And on top of that, she knows all about ostriches and somehow manages to make the crazy critters a perfect part of a perfect romance. Check this one out; you won't be disappointed.

And then come back again next month, for two more great books all about meeting—and marrying!—Mr. Right

Yours,

Leslie Wainger

Leslie Wainger
Senior Editor and Editorial Coordinator

Please address questions and book requests to:
Silhouette Reader Service
U.S.: 3010 Walden Ave., P.O. Box 1325, Buffalo, NY 14269
Canadian: P.O. Box 609, Fort Erie, Ont. L2A 5X3

MARY STARLEIGH

The Texan and the Pregnant Cowgirl

Published by Silhouette Books
America's Publisher of Contemporary Romance

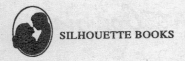

SILHOUETTE BOOKS

RECYCLED PAPER

ISBN 0-373-52068-9

THE TEXAN AND THE PREGNANT COWGIRL

Copyright © 1998 by Mary L. Schramski

This edition published by arrangement with Harlequin Books S.A.

® and TM are trademarks of Harlequin Books S.A., used under license. Trademarks indicated with ® are registered in the United States Patent and Trademark Office, the Canadian Trade Marks Office and in other countries.

Printed in U.S.A.

About the author

I've always loved words and the images they create. Three words that have had a remarkable impact on my life are *hope, love, romance.*

With *hope* I raised a beautiful daughter and just recently watched her graduate from pharmacy school.

With *love* in my heart, I met and married an exciting air force fighter pilot—the man of my dreams.

With *romance* I created J.D. and Kate for Silhouette's Yours Truly line and fulfilled a lifelong dream of writing a romance novel.

The idea for *The Texan and the Pregnant Cowgirl* came about because I live in a small Texas town north of Fort Worth. What better atmosphere for a romance than star-filled Texas nights and warm, sensuous days?

The Texan and the Pregnant Cowgirl encompasses and blends hope, love and romance. I trust you will enjoy reading J.D. and Kate's romantic story as much as I enjoyed writing it.

Sincerely,

Mary Starleigh

To my daughter,
who taught me the real meaning of love.

Acknowledgment:
Thank you to Peggy and David Tennyson,
who told me all about ostriches.

1

Click.

J. D. Pruitt pumped his shotgun and leveled the barrel at the form moving around the small car. No one came to the Circle C at midnight unannounced. It just wasn't the Texas way unless the person had a suicide wish.

He'd been enjoying a good dream, which included a naked woman and passionate, steamy sex, when the unfamiliar sound of a car's engine and the crunch of gravel had broken through his sleepy mind. In two seconds he'd pulled on his Levi's, grabbed his shotgun and shoved a flashlight into the waistband of his jeans.

The shadowy blob topped with what looked like a baseball cap opened the passenger side door. J.D. followed with the gun barrel. Hoping to get a better view of the situation, he waited for the car's interior light to flash on.

Just darkness.

Circle C had been vandalized a week ago. The robbers hadn't taken anything since there was very little in the house, but they'd sure made a mess looking for anything of value. The sheriff warned him poachers were in the area, and now he had one in his gun sight.

He was mighty upset at being woken up. It would be hours before he could call the sheriff, get this guy locked up and hit the rack again. Five a.m. came pretty early with a few hours' worth of sleep. Since Charlie died, there was double the work and no extra help.

Moving stealthily across the yard, J.D. kept his gun leveled. The intruder was short, skinny, too, except for the pot belly. When he was fifteen feet away from the car, he stood motionless and thought better of pulling the trigger. There'd be questions. He didn't relish the idea of blowing somebody's kneecap off even if the creep had come out to his property to steal eggs or chicks.

The shadowy figure pulled a knapsack over his shoulder and turned.

"That's far enough," J.D. growled. "Don't move and you'll keep your head in one piece."

A soft, crisp gasp escaped from his target. J.D. raised a brow. *Wimpy voice for a poacher.* Keeping the gun level, he traversed the last ten feet as the silhouette held perfectly still.

"Keep your hands where I can see them," J.D. yelled, and held the shotgun with one hand, the butt braced against his side. He whipped the flashlight out of his waistband, clicked on the high-powered stream of light and pointed it in the intruder's face.

Large, blinking eyes stared back at him. A much too perky nose and full mouth finished the picture. J.D. held the beam of light on the wide eyes. "You've got two seconds to tell me just what the hell you're doing here."

"You're blinding me." The voice was firm yet feminine, and the large eyes narrowed. "I'm Kate Owens, and I own half this property." She dropped her knapsack to the ground and a small cloud of dust sifted up through the beam of light. The beam traveled from her face to her body.

The poacher was a woman! Shining the light against her hands, he saw pink polish on well-manicured nails and no weapon.

The name rang through his mind.

Kate Owens! Hell. He'd heard his partner talk about her enough. But could Charlie have been crazy enough to leave his half of the ranch to a *woman?* Bringing the stream of light back to her face, he swallowed hard.

Fool woman almost got her head blown off.

Illuminating her fully with the cylinder of light, J.D. studied her face. It was shaped like the woman he'd been dreaming of—a perfect heart that held sexy eyes, high cheekbones, a small dusting of freckles across her nose and a mouth that looked like it might be waiting to be...

He stopped himself. He was much too angry to finish off the fantasy. J.D. crisscrossed the light down her body. It was definitely womanly. Slender, graceful shoulders, well-rounded breasts, large belly as big as a basketball, and nicely shaped thighs curving out from shorts.

A belly as large as a basketball!

J.D. ripped the beam back to her middle.

Damn! He'd almost shot a pregnant woman! Another crest of anger rose to his throat, and he brought the light up to her face. "What the hell are you doing out here in the middle of the night roaming around like this is a shopping mall?''

She squinted again, and he averted the light from her eyes and lowered the shotgun.

''Guess I could ask you the same darned thing. But I didn't happen to pull a gun on you.'' Her voice was soft even though it had a direct edge to it. The feminine lilt headed straight to his head and brought back a sharp memory of his dream. ''Who are you, anyway?''

''J. D. Pruitt.'' His sweaty palm slipped against the gun. He'd never pointed a gun at a woman before, and he certainly didn't like starting now.

''If you'd bother to answer your phone you would know I was on my way out here. I've called you fifteen times.'' Her lips formed into a pout.

''So you're the one that's been calling and hanging up. This is the nineties. Ever think about leaving a message?'' He let his eyes travel over her again. Her body relaxed a little when the gun wasn't pointed at her.

Kate laughed cynically at his words. ''Listen Mr.—''

''Pruitt, but you can call me J.D.'' She was feisty. Most people he knew wouldn't be laughing after having a double-barreled shotgun pointed at them.

''Mr. Pruitt, I tried to leave messages, but your answer machine cuts off. I guess I could have contacted you by carrier pigeon.''

J.D. shined the light on her just enough so he could see her face. She was awfully pretty, and he liked her quick wit. ''Probably wouldn't make its way out here, daarrliinn.'' He drawled the last word. ''But since it's after midnight, let's cut to the chase. If you're here to grab your uncle's possessions, you can forget it, he didn't have much. Couple of changes of clothes, which I gave to the Salvation Army, and some books—"

"I beg your pardon?" She quirked an eyebrow at him.

"At midnight I don't feel like any begging. I'm up at five, whether I go to bed at nine or one. I can load the books in your car, and you can be on the road in fifteen minutes—"

She laughed again, her pretty bottom lip trembling. "Fifteen minutes, I don't think so. I'm here to stay." She hooked a thumb, directing his attention to the ancient car.

J.D. pointed his flashlight and the high beam lit up the interior. Boxes filled the back seat to the roof. Obviously she was on the road to somewhere. "On a trip and thought you'd put up here for the night?" J.D. tried to keep the annoyance out of his voice, but it was difficult. After all, the woman was pregnant. But there was something about being yanked from the middle of a just-about-perfect dream where a beautiful woman—almost as pretty as the one standing in front of him—was just about to....

I better stop thinking that way, there's a lady present.

"No! I'm planning on living at the Circle C."

J.D. snorted. "Live here...at the ranch, you gotta be kidding me." He flipped the light back to her face. Why did she have to have such vulnerable eyes?

Her gaze fought through the beam to glare at him. "No, Mr. Pruitt, *I am not kidding you.* I plan to live here and help run the Circle C." With an erotic sweep, one delicate hand went up to her brow as she tried to shade her eyes and the other went to her hip. She moved with the seductiveness of a dancer. J.D.'s mind blazed with thoughts he had no business thinking.

He raised his gaze to look at her face. She wasn't kidding around. But he didn't need this woman or any woman interfering with the Circle C's daily work routine. "So." J.D. shifted his weight and crossed his arms, still holding the gun. "What we're talking about is you owning half the ranch and wanting to live here...." He stopped before he'd added, *That's the dumbest idea I've heard in a long time.* That, he knew, would only make her more upset.

"Yes. Uncle Charlie, before he passed on, wrote in his letter he thought it would be a good idea to raise my child out here in the country. He even mentioned I might like you. Imagine that!"

J.D wondered whatever made him think this woman vulnerable. With that mouth, she could protect herself from a buzz saw. But whether she was vulnerable or not didn't seem important right now.

"I don't think *that's* such a good idea." There. He'd dropped the bomb. With Charlie gone, he had more chores, more to learn about ranching and more money to make. He didn't have time to be babysitting some pie-in-the-sky female who thought she could run a ranch.

"Me liking you isn't such a good idea, true, but I'm here, and I'm here to...stay." She stomped her foot against the ground and dust floated up around her ankles. She was quick and sassy, and he found that attractive.

He snapped his gaze to hers. "I didn't mean it that way, about you liking me. Although if you got to know me you probably would." He chuckled and let his eyes roam down her legs. Great ankles, shapely calves, darn good legs....

He forced himself to continue. "The not-so-good idea has to do with you living here. Ranching is hard work, tough work. Been planning on hiring a ranch hand, let him take Charlie's room. Don't need someone around asking dumb questions and getting in the way."

The fire sparked in her eyes, and he backpedaled. "Not that you couldn't handle it, but in your condition—"

"Can we please leave my condition out of this? I'm not dying, I'm just pregnant. Women do it all the time...have babies that is." Her eyes narrowed and she stared at him. As if to accent her stand, she patted her abdomen.

Feisty, all right—the only word that could describe Kate Owens. Well, that and darned attractive when her eyes narrowed with anger and got that sexy cast to them.

"The ranch is half mine and I'm staying." Her voice had calmed a little, but a look of determination changed her face. J.D. wondered how he could have ever thought this woman susceptible to anything.

If the ranch was half hers, then she had every right to be here, but he didn't have the time or inclination to coddle a woman while she decided ranching was too difficult. He was a loner, and he liked his life that way. Women always thought they wanted something, then halfway through, they'd decide they wanted something else.

"How long did it take you to decide you wanted to be a rancher? Charlie's only been gone a few weeks.'' J.D.'s view of women had been molded into a very fine belief.

"A few days."

"Sorry. Got too much work to do around here to be showing you the ropes."

"I can help."

"Wouldn't work. Charlie and I split the chores. He did all the accounting, measuring and feeding—''

"It doesn't sound that hard."

"Don't need a female trying to learn ranching...only cause me more work and worry."

Another defiant expression grew on her face. "You don't have to worry about me."

She wasn't going to be talked out of anything easily. Now that he thought about it, J.D. remembered that Charlie had gone on and on about his Kate. How smart, talented and determined his favorite relative was. Why hadn't J.D. realized that this woman was the next of kin Charlie had decided to leave his share of the Circle C to? Charlie had been right about a lot of things in the years they'd known each other. But this time....

J.D. felt a trickle of sweat run down his back.

Arguing with a complete stranger, who'd pointed a gun at her and obviously never won a personality contest, wasn't Kate's idea of a good time.

She looked up at him and wasn't happy with what she saw. So this was Uncle Charlie's partner. Not that he wasn't nice to look at—he was. He was still staring at her, and although he didn't look eccentric, he had to be. Uncle Charlie's partners were always a quart low on one thing or another. Why would Mr. J. D. Pruitt be any different?

But he didn't look like Uncle Charlie's regular partners. The last one had been a self-proclaimed guru who wrapped himself in a bedsheet and shaved his head. J.D.'s dark brown hair was cut short and conservative, and it framed an all-American face anyone would say was just a shade away from handsome.

Her gaze traveled from his face to his wide bare shoulders, down his chest and then to his waist. J. D. Pruitt looked good in his low-slung Levi's and nothing else, but something had to be wrong with him....

Uncle Charlie never did normal.

She glanced back. Broad shoulders were evident. His slim hips made her remember fantasies she'd enjoyed before her ex-husband had ripped her capacity to fantasize away.

Snapping her gaze back to his face, she studied his eyes. The flashlight beam cast enough light on his face to see he had nice brown eyes that just happened to be surrounded by the thickest brown lashes she'd seen in a long time. Sexy, hooded lids blinked over his eyes. But he was Uncle Charlie's partner and that could only mean he was weird, or on his way there. Probably three cards short of a deck.

He cleared his throat and she set her mouth in a firm line, ready for the next argument.

"You ever live on a ranch before?" he asked, his voice laced with a bit of false concern.

"No...but I'm a fast learner." Determined to make a new life for herself and her child, she'd made a quick decision to leave Dallas. Now it didn't seem like such a great idea. But things happened fast in her life. Too quickly she'd found out her husband

Michael was leaving, and the results of her pregnancy test had been positive.

She took another breath to steady her nerves. Sure, she'd never lived on a ranch, never even visited one. After buying books on chicken raising, she'd taught herself quite a bit already. Uncle Charlie was the genius and inventor of the family and had taught her the best lesson in life. Books held all the information in the world.

"Why would you want to live at the Circle C in your...uh...condition?" he asked with a certain amount of patience she didn't really expect at this late hour. Her back and legs ached, and all she really wanted to do was lie down in a soft bed with her head on a clean pillowcase and go to sleep.

"My condition has nothing to do with where I live. Uncle Charlie left me his part of the ranch." She tried to bend down to pick up her knapsack but couldn't find the energy. A groan slipped from the back of her throat and she straightened.

He placed the flashlight in the waistband of his jeans and reached for her knapsack. Her eyes remained glued to the illuminated area and distracted her for a moment. The flashlight beam glanced over a slight tear in the seat of his worn jeans...the crazy man didn't even have underwear on. She quickly forced her gaze back to his face.

"Looks like you need this." He handed her the leather bag, brushing his fingers against hers.

"I could have gotten it myself. I'm just a little tired, that's all. It's been a long day." She unzipped the bag and rummaged through the paperwork she'd folded into one of the pockets. Uncle Charlie's will was at the bottom. She pulled it out and shoved it at him. "Half the Circle C is mine."

He refused to take it from her. "I believe you. All I'm asking is why would you want to live way out here? You don't look like you know a darned thing about ranching."

She repositioned her weight and dropped the knapsack again. "Dallas isn't any place to raise a child." Her hand automatically went to her belly, and she rubbed it. "I want a safe place to raise my baby." She wanted a place with values and family and love—away from the emptiness of a big city. She wanted to attach with good things, for her child.

"So you drove all the way here thinking you could live on this ranch?"

"I'm going to live on the ranch."

Nodding her head, she tried not to look scatterbrained. No way was she planning on appearing helpless. She squared her shoulders the best she could and raised her chin.

"And what about Mr. Owens? He want to live in the country, too?" J.D. pulled the flashlight out of his pants and shined it on the car as if to find a *mister* in the back seat hiding behind the boxes.

"There is no husband. Just me and in two months a little me. I'm hoping for a girl."

"No mister, huh?" He didn't wait for any reply before he started his lecture. "You shouldn't be out on a lonely road at midnight about to have a baby." He studied her and twisted his mouth in a funny grimace.

Kate's head started to pound. He was already starting to push her around, and he didn't even know her. The way his eyes squinted and his mouth set in a thin line told her he felt sorry for her because she was alone.

She lowered her head and laughed. Part from sheer exhaustion and the other from familiarity. Men had a way of taking control and telling women what to do, as if a woman didn't have a brain in her head—and Mr. J. D. Pruitt was obviously no different. The defect had to be from the missing line on their chromosomes.

Two *X*'s were surely more powerful than an *X* and a *Y*. The male was missing one-fourth of what a female possessed. Or maybe it was the male hormone thing. She'd read testosterone did strange things to the mind and body.

She lifted her eyes and held his gaze, studying his thick-lashed eyes. He sure acted like a normal male—*bossy as hell.*

J.D. ran the edge of the flashlight down his jaw. The intensity of the light cast sharp shadows across his face and for a moment Kate felt a shiver run up her spine. For the first time she wondered what in the world she *was* doing out in the middle of nowhere, talking to a total stranger who might just be crazy.

Suddenly a terrorizing thought jumped in. What if this wasn't her uncle's partner? She automatically placed a protective hand over her belly. The baby rolled inside her.

"How do I know you're who you say you are, anyway?" She glared up at him, trying to work defiance into her stare. If she wanted to do things for herself, there was no time like the present. All she really wanted was to run the ranch herself. She studied J.D. She didn't need a half-crazy lunatic around.

He chuckled. "You don't." His mouth curved into a lazy grin.

"Maybe you're lying and saying you're my uncle's partner. Give me some proof."

Another chuckle. "You come here at midnight, wake me out of a sound sleep and interrupt a nice dream, and you want me to give you proof I'm who I say I am?"

But she had her rights, too. "Well, how do I know?"

"Take my word for it, I'm your uncle's partner, or was. Who else would be out here arguing with you?" He smiled.

He did have a point. Who else would be standing naked but for a pair of jeans, arguing about who he was with a stranger? Only Uncle Charlie's partner.

Feeling safe again, her hand went to what used to be her waist, and she pressed her fingers into the small of her back.

He glanced down at her with a curious look on his face. "Backache?" he asked, and she thought she detected a bit of sympathy.

"No." Her back did hurt, and the baby was moving around so much she thought she might wet her pants any minute. "I do need to use the ladies' room, though."

Suddenly a groaning, moaning, *not-anything-she'd-ever-heard-before-in-her-life* noise made her jump. It sounded like a clogged trumpet announcing a scary movie. She shivered and crossed her arms. "What was that?"

"One of the roosters." J.D. kept his gaze on her. Kate felt her eyes grow large, and she stared back at him. *He was serious.*

She'd never heard any chicken make a sound like that. But she was too tired to even question his answer. She sighed.

Just her luck! J. D. Pruitt was three floors short of a building.

2

"We'd better get to bed," J.D. said as he picked Kate's knapsack off the dusty ground. "Too late for you to be going anywhere." As he shook her bag, dust scattered. "This all you'll be needing in the house?"

"There's a suitcase on the passenger seat." Kate started for it. He gripped her arm. Strong fingers worn with calluses wrapped and pressed against her flesh.

"I'll get it. Why don't you go on into the house? The front door is open," J.D. growled.

She turned to face him, knowing if she didn't stand up for herself now, it would be too late. Education 101 had taught her that much. Take control early or lose it forever. She shook his arm away. "I can get my own bag. I might be pregnant, but I'm not an invalid." She marched to the car, not giving him a chance to answer.

The bag seemed to weigh more than it had this morning when she'd put it in the car. For a fleeting moment she wished she wasn't quite so independent. She settled the wide strap over her shoulder and walked back to J.D. "I'm ready. Which way?"

"Follow me," was all he said, and turned toward

the house. He lit the path with his flashlight in one hand, her knapsack strap over his shoulder and his shotgun in the other hand. In the dim light, she studied his gait. He had a direct, no-nonsense walk, and his strong legs carried his large, muscular body without a problem.

When they reached the door, J.D. tucked the flashlight into his waistband again, turned the doorknob and pushed on the oak with his shoulder. Stopping to wipe her feet on the welcome mat, Kate followed him through the door.

"It's not much, but it's home."

The house was small and neater than she expected. The living area held a plaid Herculon couch, chair and two tattered lamps on very old end tables. Three boxes of books sat in the corner. Kate suspected they were her uncle's, and she blinked back salty tears.

Although neat, the room was devoid of personality. The walls were sterile like a hospital, missing pictures or other mementos. The emptiness created a cold environment without feeling. The only homey touch was a braided rug on the hardwood floor in front of the couch.

"I see you're into minimalist decorating," she quipped as she gazed around the room again.

"Not much time for decorating around here. Ranching consumes all waking hours." Worry lines formed on his forehead making him a little too handsome. Kate drew her gaze from his face.

A modest dining area off the kitchen was visible to the left, and on the right, an opening to the hallway where the bedrooms must be.

"A picture here and there would take all of two minutes to hang."

He chuckled. Any remnant of a frown disappeared, and a smile took its place. ''And then we'd have to have plants and pretty soon a frilly pillow on the couch and a doily here and there....''

Through her apprehension, an inner laugh was growing. Even if he was crazy as a bedbug, at least J. D. Pruitt had a sense of humor. ''Well you don't need to get carried away, soon you'll be talking about percale and organdy.''

''Maybe lilac throw pillows and a nice crocheted blanket on the couch,'' he joked.

Kate bit back a smile. ''I might be able to spruce things up a bit.''

J.D.'s grimace was back. ''You can take your uncle's room for now. Sheets are clean, and there's plenty of towels in the bathroom down the hall.'' He nodded toward the hallway and walked with her knapsack to it. Reaching his hand around the door-jamb, he flipped on a light and stood aside to let her pass through. ''It's not much, but it's clean.''

She stepped into the tiny bedroom. After placing her overnighter on the floor, she looked around. The austerity reminded her of the living room. A double bed with a plain chenille bedspread sat in the middle, accompanied by a night table with a small lamp, and a battered dresser. The hardwood floors were exposed and dull. Any signs of her uncle were gone. She turned back to J.D. ''I see you and Uncle Charlie spared no expense on decorating in here, either.''

''What is this with you and decorating? You do it for a living?'' In such a small, enclosed space his rich, virile tone was more evident.

''No, I'm—I was a teacher. There were a lot of cutbacks in the district I worked in.'' Her eyes wandered around the room again. Somehow she hoped to conjure the memory of her uncle Charlie. Knowing this had been his bedroom made her sense she might be able to feel close to him again.

J.D. cleared his throat, and she glanced back. "He didn't have much. The books out in the living room are the ones I was talking about. Charlie was a good man. We got along fine. He sure thought a lot of you."

Kate inhaled, wishing she could see her uncle again. He'd always been there for her when times got tough. She turned to face J.D. They were within inches of each other. With his bare shoulder braced against the jamb, he took up most of the opening. His dark brown hair shined against the overhead light, and the smooth skin on his chest, accented by tufts of curly chest hair, stretched taut. He was tanned to a wonderful nutmeg. Without the eerie flashlight and the dark stillness surrounding them, J.D. was almost princely.

Her common sense told her she should be afraid. But for some unknown reason, she wasn't. She felt safe, comfortable and content. He gazed down at her, and she could smell his scent—a woodsy, cinnamon aroma that made her think of fireplaces and hot chocolate.

Kate shrugged her shoulders. What in the world was wrong with her? She'd just met this man. She should be scared out of her wits, locking the door and dragging the dresser in front of it.

"You mentioned you might need to use...." J.D. cocked his head toward the hall. He wore a look of downright embarrassment on his face, and for the

` first time in a long time, empathy sprang inside of her.

"Where'd you meet Uncle Charlie?" Concentrating on J.D. was all she could think of now. She tried to interrupt the uncomfortable thoughts. She didn't want to feel empathy for any man.

"Came out to the ranch and approached me about a business proposition. Liked his ideas, so we became partners. His brains, my brawn." J.D. made a fist and bent his arm at the elbow, forming a large bicep. Tawny skin stretched tight around mounded flesh, accenting the stratified bulge. The sight of J.D.'s show of maleness forced Kate to draw her gaze back to his face.

"He taught me...a lot, too," she added.

"Charlie helped get this ranch on its feet. Doing all right now, and I don't want..."

She knew exactly why he hesitated, and her hand sliced through the air. "You don't need to worry."

"Well, in this size house and with all the work to be done on the ranch, it's difficult—"

"I plan on staying out of your way." She stepped to the door.

Anticipating her move, he shifted forward to allow her to pass, and they bumped head-on into each other. J.D.'s large, square hands and strong arms went around her shoulders to steady her.

The warmth from his body felt foreign yet consoling. "Excuse me," she gasped.

His breath brushed her cheek as his chest heaved. "Pardon me." His arms tightened slightly. Kate broke the circle and took two steps back.

"Like I said, got tight quarters here. We'll talk about living arrangements later." He ripped out the words impatiently, his arms crossing over his chest, his jaw jutting, then he stepped into the hall. "Bathroom's the one on the left. I'm next door to you."

She nodded and started down the hall.

"Kate."

She paused and turned, surprised at how her heart was racing. She wrote it off to nerves and fatigue.

"You might need your overnight bag," he stated before disappearing into Uncle Charlie's room and then reappearing with her suitcase. He took the few steps to reach her.

"Thank you." Their hands touched as he passed the bag to her.

"I'm going back to bed and try to get a couple of hours' sleep. I get up at five."

"I'll be up," Kate offered, but saw another frown grow on his face. He mumbled three words she couldn't understand, then turned and took the few large steps to reach his room. Without a glance to her, he walked in and shut the door.

She stared at the white-enameled wood.

J. D. Pruitt was not an easy man to understand. But from her experience she'd never found one who was. Why had Uncle Charlie written in his letter she'd like J.D.? He knew her better than that. The man was a big grump.

Remembering her uncle always had his reasons for what he did and said, Kate shrugged.

Four fifty-five.

The digital clock flashed the numbers, and J.D turned the alarm off before it sounded. Climbing out of bed, he stretched his tight body. A full night's sleep would have been nice. He pulled on his jeans and headed toward the kitchen. The house was quiet as he started the coffee and padded back to the bathroom.

A hot shower served to wake him up a little more. He dressed quickly and went back to the kitchen to pour himself coffee. Standing at the sink sipping the hot brew, he looked out the window. His houseguest's old sports car was still parked where she'd left it last night. She hadn't split early this morning.

Taking another sip of coffee, he chuckled. No, she wasn't the type to turn chicken and slink out in the morning darkness. He'd become aware of that part of her personality last night when she'd stood up to him. Already he knew a little bit about the woman who slept in the bedroom next to his.

She wasn't the type that gave up easily.

And she was determined to become a part of the ranch. The resolute look on her face told him that…and other things. Like how her eyes could look innocent one minute and damned sexy the next. And her mouth, the way it parted in surprise and grew into a smile that served as pure radiance. But her staying at the ranch wasn't going to work. He didn't need to worry about a female getting in his way.

J.D. picked up the coffeepot and filled his mug again. He'd finish drinking the morning brew and then head on out. Collecting the eggs, cleaning out the pens, tapping shells that were too tough to crack and vaccinating the chicks would take up his entire morning. Later he'd get some bookwork done.

At lunchtime he'd sit down with Kate and offer to buy her out. He'd use the solid argument about the house being small, and how he needed to use the extra bedroom for a ranch hand who could help him.

Moving back to the kitchen window, he watched the rising sun turn the early morning shadows into familiar objects. He'd pay her a fair price and wish her well. She could go find herself a teaching job in some small town, have her baby and live happily ever after.

Without getting in his way.

"Good morning."

J.D.'s gaze shifted and he blinked. He didn't expect Kate to be up at five. But she stood in the hallway staring at him across the living room. She was wearing a green nightgown that was modest enough. The unique shade enhanced her ivory skin and showed its vibrancy. Her face looked soothed and well-rested. She'd brushed her auburn hair away from her face, and it fell to her shoulders in wavy ribbons. In the light of the hallway she looked like a breathtaking picture of a woman with child—radiant and alluring.

"Morning." He averted his eyes and wished she didn't look quite so captivating. "I made coffee. Do you drink it in your condi—" The idea of being attracted to a woman who just happened to be pregnant surprised him. He'd never been in a situation where he was in such close quarters with a someone who was so close to having a baby. But with Kate standing in the morning light, looking pretty mesmerizing, the idea seemed plausible.

He shook his head. Charlie's death and extra chores must be working on his brain. He revised his question. "Coffee?"

"Is it unleaded? I'm trying to stay away from caffeine."

"Nope. At five in the morning I need all the help

I can get. But there's some instant decaf Charlie used to drink at night, if you want some.''

"Please don't go to any trouble.'' She waved her delicate hand in an effort to stop him. "Do I have time to take a shower? I'll be ready in just a few minutes.''

"Go ahead. Water's nice and hot.'' He nodded toward the hallway and in an instant she was gone. He stepped to the sink and filled the teakettle with water then placed it on the stove.

As the water began to boil, Kate walked into the kitchen. She'd washed and braided her hair, and it smelled clean and minty. Her cheeks without makeup glowed. She was dressed in a large white shirt, shorts and hiking boots.

J.D. stirred the granules of instant coffee in Charlie's mug, glancing at his new houseguest. Although she was far along in her pregnancy, he noticed she had an exquisite look about her. The only extra weight she seemed to carry was in her tummy area. "Take it black?'' he asked.

"Black's fine. Thanks for making the coffee. I did want some but didn't want to put you out.'' She took the mug and sipped. "Good.'' Her green eyes sparkled at him over the rim.

"Sleep well?'' J.D. asked.

She nodded.

His heart paced with the ticking of the clock on the wall. "I need to get started. I'll be back at noon, and we can talk about this situation.''

"Wait a minute.'' Kate placed her mug on the counter and glanced up at him. "I didn't get up before the chickens to sit around the house. I was planning on starting to learn the business today.''

"Your pretty white blouse is going to get mighty dirty." Tugging on her shirttail, he tried to smile. Although he didn't want her in the way, he admired her gumption.

"I expected it to get dirty, working on a ranch. It's the only top I have that's big enough. I've exploded the last few weeks." She pressed her hands to her belly.

J.D.'s gaze followed her hands. He and his wife Ann had never had time to talk about having children. They'd always been so busy earning a living. And then before they could decide, it was too late. He tried to smile again. "I think it's better you stay in the house. You could go through your uncle's books and decide which ones you want...."

Her eyes narrowed into the look he'd witnessed last night. Her lips formed a half pout, forcing a jagged desire in him, and he wondered how they would feel against his mouth.

Keep your mind on the problem at hand, J.D., his realistic side prodded before he let his imagination go any further.

"I want to see the ranch and now is as good a time as any. I promise I won't get in the way. And I might even be some help."

She was right. As soon as he showed her the hard work and the amount of it, the better off they'd both be. She might even hightail it back to Dallas. "You've got a point there. Not the help part, ranching is tough work, but you do deserve to see the Circle C. It's part yours." He finished his coffee and rinsed his mug. "Anytime you're ready," he stated as he studied her.

She stood staring at him, her hands on her hips.

Obviously Kate was a no-nonsense type of woman who had her mind made up. That and her sensuous mouth and green eyes added up to a pretty nice package. He quickly chastised himself again.

The lady's going to have a baby, and is probably heartbroken over the guy who got her that way.

She drained her mug and rinsed it. Turning to him, she offered a big smile. "I'm ready when you are."

Kate looked out the kitchen window and admired the country scenery. She'd gotten a good night's sleep despite the short hours. With the rest and beautiful sunrise she knew she'd made the right decision coming to the Circle C.

But last night, after she'd climbed into bed, she wondered if J.D. was crazy. This morning as she stood in the foreign kitchen waiting for him, she silently laughed at the outrageous thought. No, he wasn't dangerous, she knew that much. But he was different.

J.D. walked back into the kitchen. He'd put on a work shirt and a cowboy hat, and she was quickly riveted to dark eyes that looked incredibly sensual under the dark brim of his hat.

"Need a hat to keep the sun off your face when it comes up all the way." She took his suggestion and went to her room, found her baseball cap and pulled it on.

Silently they walked out the back door. The morning was fresh with spring. The baby turned gently, and she read it as a sign that her son or daughter was happy with her decision to move to the country. She smiled to herself, patted her belly and quickened her step to catch up with him.

"Beautiful day, isn't it?" She walked alongside him, lengthening her stride.

He looked down at her, the corners of his mouth lifting in a grin. "Yeah, spring's like a new beginning. Summer, that's the killer. Hot as hell, but you should know, you're from Dallas, right?"

She nodded her head. "I don't like the city, that's why I'm here."

He looked down again, smiled and slowed his pace. "No, you don't look like a city gal."

"Dallas is fine, but this is better."

J.D. stopped two hundred feet from the house and pointed in front of him. "The fence starts the pens."

The tall Cyclone fencing divided the property into parcels. She surveyed the area and then turned back to J.D., and he continued. "Birds are kept in pens. Ranch has fifty pairs."

They continued walking down the dirt path. Kate looked into the first pen. Two ostriches stood staring back at her. "Where did those come from?" Kate pointed to her new audience.

"Kenya, East Africa. Those two were our first ones."

Kate sucked in a breath. "But they're ostriches!"

He faced her, another smile growing. "Very observant. Passed biology with flying colors?"

"Actually I did quite well, but anyone would know those aren't chickens. They're too tall." The birds craned their necks, their large glasslike eyes keenly aware of the humans.

J.D. snorted a laugh. "Chickens! Never had any chickens on the Circle C. I started with beef, but when your uncle came along with the idea of raising ostriches... I may not be a genius, but I'm not a dummy, either. Ostriches are moneymakers,'' J.D. stated.

Kate tore her gaze away from the birds and looked up at him. He was serious.

"You thought this was a chicken ranch?" Another grin grew on his face. "With poultry?"

"Yes, I did think we'd be raising chickens. Familiar, home-grown poultry that didn't look like characters from *Jurassic Park*. Uncle Charlie wrote me once about hens and roosters, chicks and eggs, but I thought he was talking about chickens. Everything I've read has been about how to take care of chickens, not those... Why, they're bigger than I am." Dropping her chin, she eyed the birds again. Pictures certainly didn't do the ostriches justice. They were awesome.

J.D. laughed. "Just think of them as big chickens. Actually they're better. Not as smelly and dirty. Plus they aren't disease-prone. They hardly ever get sick and they live for fifty, sixty years. Their meat is low cholesterol. But if they don't produce...." His hand drew across his throat.

"Produce what?" Kate tried to keep her eyes their regular size, but she felt them grow wide again.

"Most people raise them for meat, but we keep the birds to produce chicks. Then we ship the hatchlings out to buyers. A prolific couple can produce a fertile egg every other day." The early morning sunrise bit at the dark. The soft hues outlined J.D., putting a glowing aura around him.

She added up the eggs. "A fertile egg...every other day, that means...." She stopped and looked at the pair in the first pen. Ostriches certainly enjoyed themselves.

"Yep! They sure do," J.D. announced as if reading her mind.

"So all they do is produce eggs? Seems easy enough."

A chuckle slipped from J.D. "Yeah, real easy! Guess we'd better get started. Need to get the egg cart first."

One of the ostriches bellowed, and drew Kate's attention. It was the same noise that had scared the heck out of her, and she wondered if she'd ever have the nerve to go into the pens. "That's the sound I heard last night."

J.D. retrieved a large cart that sat to the side of the fencing and marched down the path. "Called 'booming.' They use that and 'candling,' twisting their necks, to get their lady love's attention. Supposed to make the little woman amorous. Kinda like humans, don't you think?"

"Whatever you say." She kept pace with him down the path and listened intently as he spoke about working around the ranch.

"Eggs have to be collected twice a day. Usually the hens lay at night." He stopped at the first gate, opened the latch and entered. Kate waited and watched J.D. He shooed the large birds away and went to what looked like a small crater in the dusty earth. Coming back, he carried an egg the size of a head of iceberg lettuce. "It's heavy." He handed it to Kate. She held the egg with both hands, lifting it up and down, feeling the weight.

J.D. nodded to the egg cart. "Most eggs weigh about three pounds. They need to be collected and put in the incubator."

Kate placed the still-warm egg carefully on the straw that lined the cart.

"After collecting the eggs, the pens need to be cleaned out, then the birds need to be fed and watered. I usually spend the afternoon in the hatching barn working with the chicks."

She listened, working hard to remember it all. "How long does it take to incubate an egg?"

"Forty days. We have an incubator that holds a hundred eggs. And it's full all the time. Contraption also turns the eggs so the yolks don't stick to the shells. That's why we don't leave them in the nests. Birds have a natural instinct to roll them around, but they tend to get cracked." He stopped and looked down at her seriously. "Find this interesting?"

She nodded. "I think it's fascinating. Since I only studied books on chickens, everything is new to me." She stared at the next set of birds. They looked the same as the first—goofy.

"When your uncle came to me with the idea of raising ostriches, I was totally against it," he said before he unlatched the gate and entered the pen.

She stood by the fence and J.D. came back with another egg. "This one's huge." He placed the beige oval in her open hands.

"Beautiful." Kate rolled the egg between her hands and admired the perfect shape and the grainy texture of the shell.

"Thought you'd be queasy 'bout this stuff." He smiled down at her and continued. "Charlie showed me the figures, and I couldn't believe how much money we could make on these weird-looking guys."

They walked easily in front of the pens, the morning light bathing them in softness. Kate was surprised at how comfortable she was in J.D.'s company compared to last night. Working seemed to put him at ease. Some of the chores he'd just told her about, she was sure she could do. None of them involved heavy lifting or tough physical exertion.

They stopped at the next pen, and she gazed at the new set of birds. "Do they have names?"

"Nah."

Her finger pointed to the pair. "They need names." Walking to the fence, she curled her fingers around the chain link and stared at the birds.

"Didn't name them. They're livestock, not pets. But they do have personalities all their own. That rooster is pretty mean."

She propped her hands on her hips and pressed her lips together. "They need names." She shifted her gaze up the path. "That male in the last pen reminds me of Herman, a history teacher I taught with. Only he was a confirmed bachelor." She stepped back for a better vantage point, her hands still on her hips. She accidently backed into J.D. His hands instinctively rested over her own hands.

He cleared his throat and stepped back, and she missed the calm she'd felt from his firm, warm touch.

"Why in the world would you call that one Herman?" he asked, his low-pitched masculine voice rumbling through her.

"He just looks like him. The way he ducks his head—"

"They all duck their heads that way. It's called 'candling.'" Moving to the fence, he stood next to her, his arm brushing against hers. "That's the way he gets the hen's attention." They watched as the rooster swung his head back and forth, his long, skinny neck like rubber.

"All that to get her attention?" She glanced at the other bird, obviously his mate. The hen seemed to be ignoring the preening male. Suddenly she felt J.D.'s gaze on her, and she tried to ignore it, not wanting to be distracted by his dark, searching eyes. But she gave in to her pledge not to look at him.

"That's nature. A man is always trying to get a female's attention. Sometimes it works, sometimes it doesn't." His eyelids were half closed against the sun, and his cowboy hat edged his gaze. His eyes looked incredibly sexy, even though she'd tried to convince herself they weren't.

The strange noise brought her attention back to the bird. The larger ostrich who'd been twisting his head back and forth and making the strange noise was now behind the female. Not needing an explanation for what was going on, Kate turned her back quickly to the fence, heat flashing to her cheeks. She didn't want to discuss what the birds were obviously doing. To her chagrin she remembered J.D.'s hands on the curve of her hips as he'd stood behind her.

"You know, J.D., I could easily collect the eggs every morning, and the incubator work doesn't sound like it involves any heavy lifting," she said, eager to get all the attention away from things she didn't want to think about. Smiling, she waited for his answer and her hand automatically slid to his bare arm.

He looked down at her fingers and awareness seemed to emanate from their contact. Kate felt the insane urge to rise on her tiptoes and kiss his cheek softly.

The mood was quickly broken when he shrugged,

seeming distracted and irritated by her statement. She slipped her hand away and repressed a sigh. What in the world was wrong with her? She hadn't felt like kissing a man, even in the friendliest sense, in a very long time. Her pregnancy had to be doing something to her hormones.

J.D. cleared his throat and started toward the next set of birds. "Can talk about you working the ranch later."

3

Twelve hours later they sat at the kitchen table eating dinner. J.D. chewed a mouthful of rice and chicken and tried to keep a moan of satisfaction out of his throat.

Kate Owens, among other things, could cook.

He'd done all the morning chores, and she'd watched him, helping when she could and staying out of the way when she couldn't. He only had to show her once how to keep track of the eggs, and she'd worked with the incubator most of the afternoon while he'd mucked out the pens.

He hated to admit it, but with her help in the hatching barn, he'd cut three hours off his daily schedule, and now they were sitting down to a delicious dinner of baked chicken, curried rice and green beans.

Kate sat across from him seeming to enjoy her food as much as he was. They ate and talked, each commenting on the work. Kate asked serious, important questions, and he gave her answers.

Placing her fork on the empty plate, she spoke. "Did you get all your chores finished?"

"Yeah, I finished the chores early...great dinner." He studied her across the table. Her hair, still wet from her shower, hung loosely around her shoulders. She looked fresh, pretty and womanly.

His gaze traveled down the side of her face to the long curve of her neck and ended at the vee of her blouse. The rise of each breast was evident, and he wondered what they might look like with no material covering them. The inclination to touch the high, soft mounds with his fingertips nearly scalded him. He forced his eyes away, pushed a small amount of food around his plate and worked at controlling his breathing.

Kate smiled and nodded one time as a look of satisfaction grew on her face.

J.D. questioned his mood. Why did he have to be attracted to her? Was it because they were in close quarters? Maybe, but he'd always been careful about who he became involved with. Since Ann's death, he'd picked women who wouldn't be around long, ones who weren't capable of any promises—women that were just like him.

He liked his personal life that way.

Kate wasn't like the women he'd made a point of setting his sights on for a few weeks of companionship. He'd seen that today. And the fact was treacherous ground for his peace of mind. He'd worked out a simple system for himself. Don't get too close. He'd learned the trick from bitter experience—if he didn't get too close then there was no room to care and worry.

"You divorced?" he asked, almost surprising himself. In the back of his mind he was hoping she'd left her husband on a whim, and would go back to him, forgetting about the Circle C.

Her eyes darted to meet his, and he could tell he'd

astonished her with the question. She nodded her head, her voice lowering to just above a whisper. "Yes. I've been divorced for a while. My husband left me for one of his female colleagues."

J.D.'s eyes riveted themselves to her soft mouth. How in the world could she be in such control? How could a sane man leave a woman like Kate and their child? "Amicable divorce?" Certainly the man was crazy—or worse.

"No. My ex-husband is used to getting what he wants. He's remarried and wants nothing to do with us. But we'll get along just fine." She patted her abdomen gently. The tone of her voice had changed, and J.D. likened it to a mama tiger. His own fury almost choked him. Why in the hell would someone not treat her with respect?

The effect Kate caused rattled him. He had no desire to be protective of anyone, no matter how green her eyes might be, or how sweet her hair might smell. He'd been pulled through a knothole backward when Ann had died, and he wasn't about to go through any of those feelings again.

He needed to remedy this situation—fast. "You've seen the work on the ranch. Need to discuss what type of arrangement we can work out." He stopped, hoping he could read her mind.

Kate blinked twice and waited for him to go on.

"As I told you, this situation isn't going to work. I need Charlie's room for a hired hand." Clearing his throat, he pushed himself back from the table. "Might be better if I just buy your share out, and you can move along with your life."

Kate bit her bottom lip and stared at J.D. as if waiting for him to continue or take back what he just said. She didn't say a word. He half expected her eyes to get all shiny and wet and maybe burst into tears. He'd comfort her a little and then talk her into selling.

Silence wasn't exactly what he'd expected.

"Well?"

"Obviously you weren't listening when I told you last night I'm planning on running the ranch or at least helping. But if you'll accept the same deal, I'll be happy to buy *you* out." A manicured finger with marred fingernail polish pointed at his chest.

Her words stunned him. He had no intention of leaving the Circle C, either. *Women! They were the most illogical, emotional, unreasonable group…how in the hell did she plan on running the ranch with little experience….*

His mind continued its tailspin. "Why that's the craziest thing—" He stopped when he saw the fiery determination in her eyes.

She inhaled, paused, exhaled and measured her words.

"You're forgetting I own half of everything. The house, the ranch, the ostriches, the eggs and even the incubator." She stopped, laced her hands in front of her and waited.

What she said *was* true—she did own half. He'd taken a good look at the will last night before going to bed. Fifty percent of the decisions could be hers now.

"Can you handle half the work—the heavy stuff, too?" He hadn't meant to be so curt, but the words toppled out that way as he stared at her belly.

Kate didn't seem to be mad when she stood and picked up her dinner plate and walked to the sink.

Then she turned to face him. "No problem. I'll see you at 5:00 a.m."

As Kate gathered the bedcovers around her, she decided there was absolutely no way she could get along with J. D. Pruitt. He was just too domineering and chauvinistic.

She stretched her legs across the sun-clean sheets. Tired but not worn out, she sighed deeply. Working today felt good and productive and no way was she leaving the Circle C. She had enough money to buy her partner out, although it would take her entire life savings. But she knew already J. D. Pruitt wasn't a man easily moved. Stubborn would only gently describe him.

But there were other words, too.

Kate snuggled into the covers as she felt the cool night air from the open window fan across the bed. She needed to stop thinking about J.D.'s good looks, quick sense of humor and voice that lulled her into a false sense of security. Or how his hands on her own had felt good, warm and secure.

Her thoughts shot to the protectiveness he'd shown toward her when he'd held her back this morning to keep her from entering a pen without shooing the birds away first. He'd explained generously that an ostrich, if provoked, could be dangerous. A kick from a rooster held five hundred pounds of force per square inch.

Kate shivered.

She didn't need to be thinking about J.D. in any way except in business. Bossy, domineering and controlling only half described him. Traits she never wanted to see again in her life.

But when J.D. had come into the kitchen this evening before dinner with a smile on his face, smelling of soap and country air, Kate wondered if she'd judged him correctly. At times he seemed so easygoing.

In a torrent of mixed feelings, she questioned again if the pregnancy might be raising her hormones. Before coming to the Circle C, she'd anticipated the birth of her baby and running the ranch—and nothing else. She didn't need any distractions. So why had she looked at J.D. and gotten that disruptive feeling she'd vowed to never have again?

Pregnancy crazies! That's all it could be.

The sound of a booming ostrich floated through the window and met her ears. She glanced toward the open window, automatically knowing what was happening out in one of the pens. Ostriches were certainly active animals.

She brought her mind back to the problem at hand. The need to start conducting her life in a rational manner was strong. She couldn't let her heart lead her head. That's what she'd done with Michael. He'd come rushing into her life and literally swept her off her feet. And she'd allowed him to, thinking he was her knight in shining armor. She'd been so wrong.

No, she needed to be her own savior and prove she didn't need a man for anything. That she could be self-sufficient and take care of herself and the baby.

Finding out she'd failed at picking her mate and had been such a poor judge of character, had hurt. She'd felt like screaming at times, but didn't. Now she needed to be strong for her child. In her heart she'd never trust again—not like she'd trusted Michael when she'd allowed him to take over her life and be her all-consuming love.

The gentle breeze grabbed at the plain curtains covering the window and lifted them. They rose and floated toward the ceiling and then glided back to the floor only to be lifted again with the next puff of clean, country air. She'd enjoyed working with J.D. today. She liked his easy instructions and business-like manner. He wasn't a talker, didn't seem to need to be. His smile said it all. It could light up a room...or an ostrich pen.

Problem was, she could feel the excitement be-tween them.

He wanted her off the ranch. He'd made that very clear tonight after dinner. He didn't want or need her around. And why should he? A woman who could easily mess up his routine. He had his life a certain way, and no one was going to mess up *that*.

And she definitely didn't want to.

She'd had enough heartbreak with Michael. Seven months had passed, and she'd prepared herself to live her life with only her child. Self-sufficient without help from anyone. She didn't need passion or sparks or fireworks. All she needed was a decent living and a serene atmosphere for the baby.

She sighed and felt a tear, like a tiny river, run down her cheek. Would she become like the women she'd met while teaching? Single, alone and all-consumed with their children? Struggling with all the problems of raising a family by themselves, difficul-ties falling on their shoulders making them bitter and old before their time. She wiped the tears away with the tips of her fingers.

She was a strong woman, and well aware of the

dilemma she faced. She could do it—run the ranch, raise her baby to be a healthy human being and make herself happy. And she didn't need a man getting in the way. She'd prove that to him tomorrow.

"Don't think you should be lifting heavy buckets." J.D. stepped out from the pen and placed his hand over hers in an effort to take the ten-gallon bucket out of her grip. The stress in her back eased as he seized the extra weight.

"The bucket isn't that heavy," Kate argued, but let him take the alfalfa pellets into the pen and pour them into the feeding trough. They'd been working since five, just as they'd done yesterday, but today the routine was different. She'd demanded early on they split the chores and after much argument he'd agreed. Now she was feeling the heavy lifting in her back. Maybe she'd overestimated what she could and couldn't do.

J.D. sauntered out of the pen, swinging the empty bucket, and stood in front of her. "Listen, this isn't working. You're slowing me down." He took his hat off and wiped the sweat from his forehead with a red kerchief.

"Slowing you down? I thought I was helping you." Knowing she might be causing him more work, she tried to keep herself from sounding indignant. Every time she tried to do something, he'd stop what he was doing and take over.

He eyed her, his face serious. "You aren't. In your shape you don't need to be lifting heavy buckets and pulling hoses into the pens. I'm used to the birds and you're not. All I'm doing is worrying about you."

"You don't have to be concerned. I know my limitations, and I'll stop when I need to.'' She wiped at a stray tendril of hair that tickled her cheek.

''Let's cut a deal.''

''No way.'' She said she would split the ranch work down the middle and that's what she intended to do. This was the only way she was ever going to be his partner in the ostrich-ranching business.

Acting as if he hadn't heard what she said, he continued, ''If you'll take it easy and work with the eggs, I'll finish the feeding, then you can cook me dinner.'' Pausing, he waited for an answer. He didn't get one. ''It's a good trade-off.'' His large hands turned up in a pleading motion.

''It would be easier to cook this afternoon, but... No! I need to show you I can work as hard as you can. Maybe I'm not as strong, and it'll take me a few trips, but I can handle my share.''

J.D. shook his head and clucked his tongue, then handed her back the bucket. ''Have it your way. I don't have time to argue.''

Kate headed back to the storage shed where the manufactured alfalfa was kept. If she took her time, she might finish hauling the feed early this afternoon. The eggs had already been collected, and J.D. was cleaning out the pens. They could move to the incubator and work with the eggs. She wanted to learn how to take care of the chicks, too. They needed to be vaccinated and tagged before being sent to their new owners, and J.D. had promised to show her how today.

She filled the bucket and walked to the next pen. The feed really wasn't too heavy as long as she balanced the arched handle between both hands and didn't fill the bucket so full. She turned her face to the sun. Spring was her favorite time of year. It wasn't too hot or cold, she thought, and laughed. Just like the three bears. Not paying attention, her foot caught on the hose J.D. was pulling across the path, and the bucket toppled out of her hands, nuggets of feed flying everywhere. Her toes jammed against her boot and her ankle twisted.

"Whoa…whoa…whoa!" She grabbed at the fence and fell sideways. Tears sprang to her eyes from the pain.

"Kate, are you okay?" J.D. came from behind the shed just in time to hear her moan.

She swallowed hard and winced, holding back the pain. Putting pressure on her foot made her grimace again. Great. Now she'd sprained her ankle.

J.D. was standing next to her, his hand cupped on her shoulder. "Are you hurt?"

"I don't think so." She bit off the white lie. Her ankle was already starting to throb. "I just twisted my ankle a little."

He knelt down in front of her. "Which one?"

"Right."

He reached for her calf, pushed her pant leg up and unlaced her boot. "Let me take a look."

Her cheeks flushed. Although her ankle pulsed a pain message to her brain, it couldn't compete with the embarrassment she was feeling. He'd surely think she was clumsy and not capable—just what she didn't want him to assume. He carefully pulled off her boot and slipped off her cotton sock. Another flame of embarrassment rushed to her cheeks.

J.D. was kneeling at her feet, his bare chest glistening with sweat from the morning's chores. His low-slung jeans riding on his hips showed arched hipbones. A fine, downy line disappeared into the waist of his blue jeans. Pain, combined with their closeness, made her want to moan.

She turned her head and noticed she'd left the gate to the pen open. "The pen!" She spotted an ostrich heading for the opening. J.D. had told her the perils of a bird becoming loose. How it took a half day just to corral the animal, who could run forty miles an hour.

J.D. set her foot down carefully, and Kate worried he wouldn't make it in time. She'd be responsible for him having to spend long, time-consuming hours getting the bird back into the pen.

He closed and latched the gate just in time. Holding on to the fence, Kate hopped to J.D.

"Hey, stay off that ankle," he commanded as he turned back to her. He knelt down again, his hand palming her calf, turning her leg gently from side to side. The blood pulsed and coursed through the joint and she winced.

"Looks like a sprain."

Kate sighed. The pain and swelling told her the same story.

"We need to get you up to the house." Without asking permission, he stood, then leaned down and picked her up, cradling her in his arms.

"I can walk," she argued in vain.

He carried her easily up the path past the backyard and into the kitchen. After gently setting her on a kitchen chair, he pulled another over to her and raised her leg, placing it on the seat.

"I've really done it now." Her words grew into a sigh.

"Ah, don't worry about it. I've sprained many a

thing around here,'' he said as he stood at the sink, wet a dish towel, filled it with ice, then coiled it over her ankle. The sharp cold felt good against her swelling skin.

''Ice'll relieve the pain, and by tomorrow it'll be like new. You'd better see the doc, though.''

Kate pushed herself up in the chair. ''It's not that bad. I'll be fine tomorrow or maybe even this afternoon.'' She tried to sound serious, but her tone was halfhearted.

A knowing shake of his head made her heart beat a little faster. He repositioned the dish towel and ice on her ankle. ''You need to go to the doctor. Not only for your ankle...that might be just fine tomorrow. How 'bout the little guy?'' His head tilted to her stomach, and he arched his right eyebrow.

She dropped her chin and waited for the rest of the lecture, about how he needed someone to help, and how she should be concerned about her child. But to her surprise none came. When she looked back at his face, all she saw was genuine concern.

''J.D., thanks for worrying about me, but the day before I left Dallas I had my regular office visit. I have my records to bring to the doctor in Jackson.''

A curl of his lips replaced the worry on his face.

''I have an appointment for next week,'' she added.

The smile faded quickly. ''Didn't mean to interfere, but you gave me quite a scare tripping over the hose.'' J.D.'s hands remained on her leg. ''I mean...now you can see why it won't work, you living here and all—''

''I'm sorry about falling. It won't....'' Kate tried to explain, but found it difficult with J.D.'s questioning gaze and his warm hand on her bare leg. The mixture of not being able to complete her chores and being so attracted to him made everything seem out of whack and peculiar.

"Not just you falling," J.D. said, his fingers, lined deep with callouses that seemed so much a part of him, massaged her calf. "Here you are with your leg up on the chair and me with my hand...when I should be working...."

"Then get your hand off my leg and go back to work. I'll be fine."

He pulled his hand back, but still knelt beside her. Her gaze lowered to his bare chest then to the fine line of downy dark hair that dissected his middle. She knew what his words meant. He'd felt the attraction between them, too. She adjusted her leg and winced. A frown followed.

"I'm not making a pass. That's not what I meant." The tone of his voice was impatient, and he stood.

Kate stared up at him. "I didn't say anything like that!" Of course he wouldn't be interested in her. She was pregnant, for goodness' sake. But her gaze must have given her away just a moment ago. J.D. was the kind of man who could sense things, and he sensed her feelings toward him. She had to make her emotions perfectly clear.

"I don't need you." She bit her lip. His face showed a wounded look mixed with anger. She lifted her leg in a jerky motion then groaned. Why in the world did she think she could explain the way she was feeling when she couldn't even describe it to herself?

He chuckled. "Well, we have that settled. What I'd like to know is who made you think you've got to be so damned self-sufficient?'' He leaned against the kitchen counter and waited for an answer.

Kate lifted her gaze to his, hearing the question but not wanting to answer it. ''Who did what?''

''Must have been somebody pretty close. What did they do to make you think you have to handle everything by yourself?''

''My feelings have nothing to do with the ranch and our partnership.'' She crossed her arms over her belly.

''Partners are supposed to work. When one person can't do one thing or another, then the partner takes over. Like taking care of a child.'' His nails rubbed the distinct stubble that was forming on his chin, and the scratching noise filled the silent kitchen.

Kate didn't allow her gaze to drop, and she denied to herself she was the way he was describing her. ''I don't want to discuss my personal life.'' She knew enough about him to know that he didn't believe in the partnership rule he was spouting. ''I do my share, my own thing, just like a lot of people I know.'' She tried to stay neutral.

''You do more than that, don't you?'' He waited for an answer.

''No. Is there something wrong with wanting to be independent?''

A frown crossed his face, but their gazes stayed locked. ''Yes. When it leads to getting hurt.'' He nodded to her ankle.

Kate felt a bit of remorse, and her throbbing ankle enhanced the emotion. The urge to tell someone, anyone, about what Michael had done to her, how he'd let her down, and made her want to be more independent, rose inside of her.

She wanted to tell J.D. about the hurt she'd felt when her marriage had fallen apart. She also wanted to tell J.D. that yes, she was attracted to him, but couldn't possibly let herself be. How she hadn't felt like a sexual being for so long—up until the other day when she'd met J. D. Pruitt. But trust was an awful thing to lose, and an even tougher emotion to get back.

"Let's just forget it. I need to get on the couch," she said finally, and tried to stand. Between her extra weight and her ankle, she gave up on the first try.

He took the dish towel off her ankle and put it on the counter. Then he reached for her and helped her up. Before she could protest, she was in his strong arms again, her right cheek against his smooth, moist skin. He smelled good—manly without a hint of anything unnatural. Her heart skipped a beat, and she damned the erratic heartbeat.

"Thank you." She tried to keep the breathlessness out of her voice. He walked to the couch, put her down gently, and then gazed at her. Without a word he disappeared and returned with the ice, a light blanket and pillow.

"Suggest you rest for the day. I can finish up. And then I'll make us dinner. Tomorrow I'm going into town, and you can go with me. Maybe see the doc."

Her ankle throbbed and sent a dull ache up her leg. She wanted to pull the blanket over her head and sob like a kid—she was so mixed up. It felt incredibly good to have someone concerned about her. Yet she needed to get on with her life and learn about the Circle C. But being cared for right now was comforting. There were times she grew tired of doing it all.

"Didn't mean to say or do anything that might upset you," he said, then raked his hand through his hair. "I hope your ankle feels better. We can work this thing out."

"Do you think so?" she asked, hoping they might, but knowing they wouldn't be able to. They both had their own agendas and neither included the other. How simple it would be if they could come to an agreement. How easy if she didn't feel the attraction she was feeling right now. The thought scared her to death.

You're not attracted to him, you fool, she reminded herself. *It's just your crazy hormones careening out of control like some runaway train you can't stop.*

She needed to get her life in order before the baby got here. She certainly didn't want to leave the ranch. Where in the world would she go? And if a stranger could disrupt her well-thought-out mantra, then it was pretty flimsy. She needed to be strong.

"Yeah, like I said, I've had plenty of sprains, you'll be fine." His hand went to his hair again, and his fingers combed it off his forehead. "Just take it easy."

"I will," she answered, automatically shifting her gaze. She didn't want to look at him anymore. She felt like an empty-headed, frivolous woman. Tears welled in her eyes again and she pressed them back.

"Ankle hurt?" He took one step closer.

She quickly shook her head and held up her hand like a stop sign. "It'll be fine. You need to get your work done." Her tone was more harsh than she'd anticipated, but she didn't need J.D. so close while she was feeling so helpless. "I just need to be alone."

"Fine." He held her gaze for a long moment, then turned and left the room.

4

"**Y**ou're healthy, Mrs. Owens." The doctor turned toward Kate but continued making notes on her chart.

"Please call me Kate, Dr. Graham."

Meg Graham smiled and nodded her head once. "Fine, if you'll call me Meg. Everybody in town does. We're pretty informal around Jackson."

Kate liked Meg the moment she met her and was happy to know she'd be delivering her baby.

"Who would you like me to list for notification in case of an emergency? It's better if it's someone close."

She hesitated. There was no relative or friend close by, only J.D. She was sure he wouldn't want to be bothered, but she didn't have any other choice. "J. D. Pruitt. Out at the Circle C. We're partners."

Meg's gaze snapped to hers and then she laughed. Placing the clipboard on the small instrument table, she put her hand on her hip. "So you're Charlie's relative. James Dean must have been pretty darned surprised to meet you."

"James Dean?" Kate questioned.

"J. D. Pruitt is my cousin. He didn't tell you?"

She shook her head, embarrassed. Her partner had

brought her to Meg Graham's office but never mentioned he and the only doctor in town were related.

Meg stepped forward and placed her hand on Kate's shoulder. "Don't take it personally. He's always been closed-mouthed, even as a kid. And stubborn as a mule. Always has been. We need to discuss your delivery. Get dressed and meet me in my office."

She nodded, pushing herself off the examining table. "I'd like to get the arrangements made as soon as possible," Kate said, acknowledging a feeling of excitement. As much as she wanted a child, she didn't mind the idea of not being pregnant.

Meg pointed to Kate's leg that she'd just examined. "Need any help getting into my office?"

"It's all right. I can walk now without it hurting." She stepped down and put her full weight on her ankle to prove her point.

"I'll see you in a few minutes." Meg pulled the door shut and Kate dressed hurriedly.

"Have a seat." Meg made a motion to the chair in front of the unpretentious desk. "From my examination and calculations, I think your delivery date is off. You might be going into labor sooner than you expected."

"Sooner...I feel fine."

"Baby's starting to get into position. I don't see any real problems though, so we'll get you set up for the hospital. Facility's not very big, but you'll be well taken care of. When labor begins, come to town right away. I live out of town, but it's not far." Meg wrote in Kate's file and then looked up and smiled. "Any questions?"

"Is there a problem...should I be worried?" Kate's heart started to pound to her throat.

"No, not at all. I just think your due date is off. I predict a beautiful baby. Have you started natural childbirth exercises?"

Kate shook her head. There hadn't been time for any plans in Dallas.

"Well, since you're going to be at the ranch, maybe my cousin can be of some help?"

Her cheeks flamed. Irrational thoughts about J.D. and his touch had plagued her all night and early this morning. She'd wanted to ask her doctor about the crazy hallucinations. But with Meg's announcement that she might go into labor earlier, her well-thought-out questions were scattering like fallen leaves in an October wind. "I've got the pregnancy crazies," she blurted.

"What?" Meg's brows knitted into one.

Kate studied her face. She looked a lot like J.D. Warm brown eyes, smooth skin and dimples right under her cheeks when she smiled.

"My thoughts are...running away from me...and they're far from normal," Kate stammered as she felt her heart slam against her ribs. Just the memory of how she'd reacted to J.D.'s closeness yesterday sent a torturous heat weaving through her entire body.

"What's not normal? Feeling sad, depressed?"

Kate fiddled with a button on her shirt. How could she possibly articulate what she couldn't quite pin down herself? "No...well, I'm not sure." She had to stop and pick her next words carefully. She didn't want J.D.'s cousin to get the wrong idea. And if she wasn't careful with her words, Meg might. "Maybe

it's the move to Circle C and living with someone I
don't really know?''

''You're not worried about James Dean are you?''
Meg waited for an answer, and Kate shook her head.
''Good. My cousin really is a nice guy.''

The statement brought a quick laugh from Kate.
''When? He must have been about eight years old.''

''Yeah, I know. He can be a little salty at times.
But he's got a heart of gold.'' She leaned back in the
worn chair. ''It's not a good time for you to be worrying about anything.''

''N-no, it's not that I'm upset....'' Kate stammered. ''I'm not worried about *him*.'' She bit off the
last word. ''I'm troubled about...'' she stammered
and began again. We...I mean...I've been having
weird thoughts.''

Meg's gaze snapped to attention again.

Kate pressed her lips together, and her eyes narrowed. Now she'd really done it. Her new doctor
thought she was close to being a lunatic. ''What I'm
trying to say...is that I'm divorced, and I have no
interest in men at all...I just want to make...a life
for myself and the baby...but I find J.D. attractive.''

Kate sighed. Although it had been difficult to re-
veal her feelings, it was actually nice to have another
female to talk to. Yet she didn't dare tell Meg just
how his touch sent her heart into overdrive.

A smile drew across her doctor's face. ''I'm sure
my cousin's appealing, but you should have seen him
when he was a kid. Skinny! Goofy-looking.'' She
stopped and closed the folder. ''Kate, it's perfectly
normal to be attracted to men when you're pregnant.
I'd be concerned about you if you weren't. Your sex-

ual feelings can run the gamut, in fact, they can be very erratic—''

''Are many women attracted to him?'' The question popped out of her mouth before she could stop it. Meg probably knew quite a bit about J.D.

''He's had his share of girlfriends. Although he didn't have too much time for dating around. He and Ann got pretty serious right after they graduated.''

''Ann?''

''I should have figured he didn't say anything about Ann, too personal. James Dean and Ann married a year after high school. About ten years now. She was killed in a car accident about five years ago.''

''Oh, I didn't realize.'' There were no pictures around the Circle C to let her know about her partner's life. She'd been too distracted by everything else to think or ask if he'd been married.

''Not your fault. He's a man of few words. Did he bring you into town?''

''Yes, he insisted. I told him I'd be all right going by myself, but...''

''You don't need to explain. The guy can be downright bullish at times.'' Meg pressed her elbows against the desktop and cupped her chin in her hands. ''What you're feeling is very normal.''

The declaration made Kate relax a little. ''I just figured it's nerves or something.''

Meg smiled, reached for Kate's hand across the desk and patted it. ''Your hormones are raging. You'll feel differently because of them.''

Kate nodded and listened, happy to hear she wasn't going off the deep end.

Meg opened Kate's folder again and poised her

pen over the paperwork. "Did you have a healthy sex drive before?"

The question made her wince and perplexed her. Erratic, pitching emotions because J.D. was around wasn't about sex, or she hoped not. "Normal, I think." She'd never thought much about sex with Michael.

"Metabolism gets out of sync when you're pregnant. If you have good skin, sometimes you'll have problems. Conditions tend to be opposite of what they were before." Meg paused and wrote something, then tapped the pen against the desk. "Everything you're feeling is common. What I'm more worried about is your ankle."

"It's fine. It isn't swollen anymore and doesn't even ache. I elevated and kept ice on it all day yesterday." Her face flamed, embarrassed at being so clumsy.

"I know it's all right, but actually I'm more troubled about how the sprain happened in the first place. Even though you're healthy, there are restrictions when you go into the last trimester. You can't be doing things that put you and the baby in dangerous situations. How'd it happen?"

"Carrying feed to the ostriches." Kate watched a frown grow on Meg's face, her brows knitting again. Quickly she added, "J.D. and I are splitting the chores around the Circle C. I'm strong—"

"Remind me to have a talk with that lunkhead. Since you want me as your physician, I'm going to start with some orders. If you don't like my bedside manner, you can fire me and hire yourself a new doctor. But I've got to warn you, I'm the only one around for about fifty miles who delivers babies.'' Meg's voice was stern. ''You're stuck with me.''

''What orders?''

''No lifting. You can do a lot of damage. You'll have to work out a schedule with my cousin. He's hardheaded at times, but he does have some reasonable qualities, or at least I thought he did.'' She stood, walked around the desk and sat on the edge.

''Okay,'' Kate conceded immediately, her heart sinking to her stomach. Nothing would make her put her baby in jeopardy. Stinging tears pooled at the corners of her eyes. She blinked them away. Damn it, she wasn't about to cry. She'd work something out.

''Problem with any of this?''

''J.D. isn't exactly happy to have me at the ranch. I'd like to stay, but I don't know how I can now. I have to do my share of the work. He's got the perfect reason to ask me to leave, and I wouldn't blame him if he did.''

''I know how hard James Dean slaves around that menagerie. You can't possibly do the same work he does. You'll have to pace yourself. Realize what you can and can't do.''

''I understand.'' She was angry at herself for not thinking in advance. Of course she couldn't keep up with J.D. in her condition. But the truth hurt. She'd have to leave the ranch, and the reality of everything that had happened the past few days made her cringe. ''Maybe I'll go back to Dallas.''

''Either you want a healthy baby or you don't.'' Meg leaned forward. ''But I don't think moving is a good idea. You're close to delivering, and it sounds like you've got enough stress in your life. You need to stay put for a while.''

''I do.'' The realistic words came out in a whisper. Her mind was spinning out of control with thoughts of how she could work on the ranch, follow Meg's rules, yet still be an equal partner.

''Is he waiting for you?''

''Out in the truck. At least I think he's still there.''

Meg chuckled. ''If James Dean said he'd wait, then he'll be there. He's dependable as all get-out, honest, too. Actually very likable if you get beyond the gruff exterior.'' Meg stuck the pen she was holding into her pocket and stood. ''I need you to fill out some medical history forms, so while you're doing that, I'm going to say hello to him. With him living on the ranch, I don't see him as often as I'd like to.'' Meg stepped behind the desk and searched through a gray metal file cabinet. ''Here they are. Three pages' worth.'' She handed Kate the forms and a pen. ''Take your time. I'll tell my cousin you'll be out soon.''

''Hey, James Dean, where the heck you been keeping yourself?''

J.D. heard his cousin before he watched her stride across the narrow sidewalk to the driver's side of his truck. With one foot cocked on the running board, she rested her elbow against the metal of the truck and kissed him on the cheek.

''Could ask you the same question, Mego. How's Kate doing?'' J.D. moved his hand to his cousin's hair and tousled it.

''Kate's fine, but she doesn't need to be lifting

buckets, tripping and spraining body parts around the Circle C. I gave her orders to do the easy stuff.''

J.D. had heard the edge in Meg's voice before. ''I told her she shouldn't be working around the ranch,'' he announced. He ignored the gut-twisting reaction in his stomach Meg's statement brought.

''I didn't say that. She can do light cleanup, and a few other things, but no heavy lifting. She's lucky she only sprained her ankle.''

''Tried to tell her, but she wouldn't listen. Now you've told her, maybe she'll be reasonable. Best for her to move into town.'' He wanted to smile but couldn't.

''Whoa. Back the truck up. I didn't say anything about Kate leaving the ranch. That's not a good idea at all. I don't want her under any more pressure. She's just moved and doesn't need to be traipsing around again.''

''But I need help at the Circle C. Not someone who needs to lay on the couch with her feet up in the air.'' J.D. thumped the steering wheel with his thumbs.

''James Dean, you're amazing.'' Meg stared at him. ''I didn't say she had to be flat on her back, although I know some men like to picture women in that position. She can work, but it has to be minimal lifting. We don't need any injuries.''

''Good reason for her to move on.'' Ever since she'd taken a spill yesterday, his thoughts had been twisting and turning inside him like a cement mixer. Sure, he wanted her off the ranch. He needed to get back to work without worries. But a kernel of emotion deep inside made him feel he'd be missing something if Kate left.

And that was exactly what he didn't like, knowing he should feel one way, but feeling another.

"James Dean, I swear. You're still as hardheaded as ever. Listen to what I'm saying. She needs to stay put for a while. Have a heart." Meg's hand patted his bare forearm and then her fingers turned into pinchers and they pulled a small tuft of arm hair like she'd done a thousand times when they were kids.

"Ouch." J.D. pulled his arm back and rubbed it. He placed his hands on the steering wheel. "You haven't done that in years."

"You wouldn't want to be the one responsible for any harm coming to that cute little baby who's about ready to pop out, would you?"

"Ah, hell!" J.D. raised his hands off the steering wheel, and then slapped them back down. "Come on, Meg, don't go using the guilt trip on me. Course you know I don't want that, but I don't need to be worried about—"

"You don't need to worry about her. She's fine. Healthy as a horse, just don't let her work like a mule."

"Hey, I tried, but she's as stubborn as I am."

"Well, then, you two have something in common. I've talked with her, and she's agreed not to do any heavy work. I'm sure you can find *something* for her to do. She needs a home right now. I get the feeling she doesn't have any other place to go." His cousin smiled.

And his stomach dropped. Of course he couldn't tell Kate to leave when Meg put everything in perspective. As much as he wanted the ranch back, he didn't want to be responsible for any harm coming to her.

"All right, just to show you I'm not a complete jackass, she can stay. But only until the baby is born, then we'll figure out something. I offered to buy her out. I'm not running a nursing home and a day care." The words came out fast—confusion made him angry.

Suddenly, happiness flashed inside him at the thought of her staying a little longer. He gritted his teeth. How in the hell could he be happy with something he didn't even want? He silently cursed the uneasiness.

Meg's hand caressed his jaw. "Thanks, James Dean. You won't regret it. Earn you a few points in heaven." Wrapping her fingers into a loose fist, she tapped him on the chin. "What a guy."

J.D. managed a smile through his bewilderment as Kate walked out the office door and crossed the sidewalk to the truck.

"Meg, I left the papers on your desk. I think I answered all the questions."

"I'm sure you did. Hey, I'd better get back to work. Glad to see you've got yourself a good partner, James Dean." Meg walked to stand beside Kate. "Now, if you'll just behave, maybe she'll stick around."

The office phone rang just as Meg was about to say something else. "Sorry, kids, gotta run." She turned back to Kate. "Don't forget what I told you. I'll stop by the ranch soon." She paused for a moment and winked. "Everything you're feeling is natural. If you have any questions, call, day or night. James Dean has my home number." Grabbing Kate's hand, she squeezed it. "Welcome to Jackson." Then she turned and quickly ran in her office.

"Ready?" J.D.'s question brought Kate's gaze up to his.

"Yes," she answered, stepping to the passenger side of the truck. J.D. reached over and pushed the door open for her. She stepped up, then scooted onto the well-worn seat.

"Good appointment?"

"Yes."

"No problems?" J.D. asked. She looked darn worried. Heck, he certainly didn't want her problems to be any of his business. He barely knew the woman sitting next to him. Trouble with sprained ankles or babies didn't fit in his life picture.

"I can't do my share of the chores." Her whispered words traveled to him. "Meg said if I lift anything heavy or do too much, I might hurt the baby. I'd never take a chance and do that," she said as the palm of her hand rubbed against her abdomen.

His stomach clenched at the sight.

She turned her head toward the open window. J.D. could see the outline of her high cheekbone and her long, sweeping, auburn lashes. The freckles that were sprinkled across the bridge of her nose from the sun were faint. She looked frightened and helpless. He tried to deny the protective surge that washed over him. Yet he craved to wrap her in his arms and tell her he'd shoulder her problems.

Shaking his head, J.D wanted to forget yesterday when Kate nestled against his chest and he'd carried her up to the house. And forget how his unwanted protective feelings toward her had turned to pure lust. It was the kind of lust that made him want to ignore memories he'd tucked away. The kind of yearnings that seared his mind when his mood was low and he was alone.

She was sweet and utterly wrong for him. Not that he had any desire for her to be right. But why had he gotten so annoyed yesterday when she'd told him she didn't need him? He gritted his teeth and swore under his breath.

Kate turned to face him, her eyes shiny with held-back tears. "If you drive me out to the ranch, I'll pack up my belongings and come back into town and go from there. I'm sure if you start looking, you can find a ranch hand. I'm not much good to you now." Her voice was strong.

Her wide-eyed determination cut right to his heart, and he shook his head in silent wonder. How could she be so confident in such a predicament? Her grit amazed him. The urge to help her, to soothe her, hold her in his arms and tell her not to worry was strong enough that he needed to lock his fingers around the steering wheel to stop himself from holding her. He glared straight ahead.

Can't worry about her. Need to take her back to the ranch, pack her things up and wish her well. His own advice thumped through his thoughts like a silent chant.

"Don't think that's such a good idea," J.D. said, then checked his watch and looked at her. "It's almost twelve. You must be hungry. Let's go home where we can discuss this while we fix something to eat." Filling his lungs with oxygen, he thought about what he'd just said. If he didn't let her stay at the ranch, he'd be the biggest bastard in the world.

Kate sat at the kitchen table, watching him. He was making sandwiches, and she hadn't offered to help. But now she wished she had something to occupy her. Even with the impending problems and the announcement from Meg that the baby might come early, an explicit thrill shot through her when she gazed at J.D.

The magnetism felt odd, yet her pulse bounded as she watched him go from the refrigerator to the counter and back again. The mixture of it all was scary and wonderful at the same time. And she wondered if she could stand the pace of the wild hormonal rampages until the baby was born. Hopefully, by then the uneven feelings would be gone, and she and the baby could go on with their lives.

"So you gonna stay?"

His attention was still on sandwich-making when he asked the question. It was direct and to the point and caught Kate off guard. Without hesitation she knew the answer.

"No!"

Without another comment, he finished making their lunch and brought it to the table. "What the heck kind of answer is that?" J.D.'s furry brows pulled into a scowl like his cousin's, and his voice held a note of frustration as he poured her a large glass of milk.

"I can't stay if I can't help with the work. That wouldn't be fair. Meg's given me the rules, and I wouldn't feel right if I couldn't pull my own weight, as much as it is." Kate patted her belly. "And I'm still growing." She shrugged her shoulders in resignation. "You won't let me buy you out, so I'll leave."

His gaze was now direct. He was a handsome

sight, even when he questioned her and made her feel uncomfortable.

Uncomfortable wasn't really the word to describe the pure, sharp slash of sexual desire raging through her. It was quickly replaced by a rush of humiliation. Being pregnant, husbandless, and just about homeless didn't lend itself to the yearnings that seemed bound and determined to bolt through every nerve every time she looked at him. She forced the thoughts out of her mind. She was just *hormonal.* She needed to be thinking about independence and providing a home for her child.

"Always give up so easily?" J.D. asked, surprise lacing through his words.

"I'm not giving up." Kate didn't bother to pace her response, not caring if her irritation showed. "I just know when I'm licked. I can't risk my baby's health."

"Meg said you shouldn't be moving around. That could be dangerous, too." His voice took on an odd tone.

"She said that to you?" she asked, wondering if he was all right.

"Yep. Doesn't think you need to be changing residences right now. Neither do I." His voice was back to normal, and he paused a moment to take a bite of his sandwich. "Good. Eat."

"And how do you propose I earn my keep?" She didn't like him telling her what to do. Yet his concern was comforting. But hadn't Michael been concerned, too, at first? He didn't answer her question, so she went on. "Sorry, I won't stay. I'll be leaving right after lunch." She looked down at her plate and wished she had more appetite. But more than that, she wished she knew where she was going to go.

"You're stubborn."

His statement snapped her gaze back up. J.D. stared at her, his expression a mixture of directness and frustration. Taking the sandwich in both hands, he took another bite and chewed carefully.

She ignored what he'd just said for a moment and took a deep sip of milk, then a bite of her sandwich. "And you're not?"

"Nope." He took another large bite of sandwich, finishing off the half. He washed it down with most of his milk. "I'm the most easygoing, flexible—"

"Right." A crescent of milk hung on his upper lip. She reached for him and the tip of her finger drew across the milky line. He looked like a little boy enjoying his noonday meal, and warm empathy flooded her body. "You've got a milk mustache," was all she could manage, wondering why her finger had touched his mouth so quickly and easily before her rational thoughts could stop her from caressing his sensual lip.

She finished drawing her finger across his skin. The manly stubble sent an odd sensation running through her body. Bringing her hand to her napkin, she hoped he hadn't seen her tremble. "There."

He licked his lips before he spoke. "Thanks." The deepness of his voice rumbled through her sensitive body. "So, you gonna stay? I think you should, if you ask me," he said matter-of-factly.

"Who asked you?" She didn't mean to sound harsh, but her emotions were in such turmoil. Annoyed with herself and him, she didn't wait for an answer. "Yesterday you couldn't wait to get me out of here. Now you don't want me to leave. I won't be pushed around.'' She shifted in her seat. She couldn't remember anyone ever making her feel so uneven—first one way then another. And she didn't like it at all.

"Meg said you should stay, and I agree. Too much stress for you to leave.''

"*This is stress*. This conversation is stress,'' she blurted.

"Why? You wanted to stay on the ranch, so stay.''

"You think you can just tell me to leave, and then tell me to stay.''

"I'm not trying to tell you anything. Just thought you'd be better staying, that's all.''

"Well, life doesn't work that way. Everything can't go your way.'' She sensed J.D. felt sorry for her and flames of humiliation blazed to her cheeks.

"Things don't always have to go my way.'' J.D.'s tone revealed he was stunned.

"Right! I'm not one of the ostriches out there you can shoo away or call back whenever you feel like it. You can't always be in control, James Dean.'' She paused, then she sliced through the sandwich and chewed furiously. Even though she was mad, the combination of bread, mayo and tuna tasted wonderful.

One dark brow arched. "Only close relatives and good friends call me that,'' he drawled, and let his lips curl into a smile.

Kate didn't feel quite so mad when she saw him grin. "I like it. Family name?''

J.D. snorted. "Hardly. My mama gave it to me. She loved James Dean, and she was a bit of a romantic. Always said my daddy looked like him.''

Standing, he picked up his plate then walked to the sink and rinsed it.

"Did your dad like the name?" Kate asked. She craved any information about the man who stood in front of her.

"My daddy was a traveling man. Took off before I was three. I don't remember too much about him. There's a picture of him somewhere around here. Probably in a drawer." J.D. stepped closer. "You got a name picked out yet?" He pointed to her stomach.

Kate shook her head. She'd thought of names. "I'm waiting until I see him or her. I'll know then."

"Good way to do it. Take your time, don't get in a hurry. Don't get your mind set on anything," he said huskily.

Kate couldn't stop herself from laughing at his suddenly easygoing attitude.

"Not mad anymore?"

"I never was." Kate told the white lie, then stood and took her plate to the sink.

"Could have fooled me." He massaged his chin with his thumb and forefinger.

"I do have a temper, but I get over it fast. I just don't like being told what to do. I've had enough of..." Her voice trailed off and she shrugged. "Guess I am a little stubborn." She turned to face him, leaning her hip against the sink.

"So I noticed. Unfortunately, I am, too." J.D. took a step toward her then cupped her shoulders with his hands.

It felt perfectly natural for him to touch her. Nice and warm and caring. His fingers massaged her muscles absently, and her skin absorbed his warmth.

His chest expanded as he inhaled. "Look,

Kate…'' He leaned forward, bringing his head down close to hers, his mouth half open. They were so close she could see stubble on his upper lip that she'd felt with the tip of her finger a moment ago. The out-of-control feelings to get closer to him surged again.

She twisted away from him and took three steps to the side. The baby moved gently inside her. Her heart pounded up to her throat. The quick, nervous energy his closeness caused made her mouth go dry. She lifted her gaze to find he was still staring at her.

''I don't think you should move, that's all I was trying to tell you.'' The edge of his voice cut through the room.

He was right, but she didn't want his pity or charity. And she certainly didn't want him telling her what to do. She needed space and time to straighten out all her feelings. Time to think of her baby. J.D. was standing so close, ripping all the rational ideas from her mind.

She sighed. Most of all, she didn't want to feel the way he made her feel when he touched her and stood so near.

Yet Meg wanted her to stay put. She really didn't have a choice.

''Only if I can help.'' She watched as the glint came back into his eyes.

''It worked out all right the other day when you helped with the eggs in the hatching barn. Saved me a lot of time. That's not difficult, but it's important.''

''Well, if you think I can be of some help.''

''Then it's set. You're staying,'' J.D. stated. ''For a while anyway.''

5

"**N**o way, Meg. That's asking way too much of any man," J.D. declared, then stole a look at his cousin over the newspaper he'd been reading.

Meg snatched the paper from his hands, folded it neatly and replaced it with a colorful booklet titled, "Lamaze—The Natural Way."

"Come on, J.D., you're the perfect person. You might even enjoy it."

Without looking at the booklet, he handed it back to his cousin. "Don't think so. Never heard of this Lamaze stuff and don't intend on learning. And by the way, five-thirty in the morning isn't the best time to talk me into anything." His cousin had surprised him by tapping on the door a half hour ago.

"Sorry about the early hour, but I've got a busy day. When would you like to talk?" Meg tried to hand him back the booklet, but he ignored her.

"Never."

Meg laughed. "Never is not a very good time frame. She could have the baby any day now."

"Why can't you do it?"

"I can't be her coach because I'm the doctor, re-member?" Meg drained her coffee cup and held it out. "How 'bout some more? Stop fighting me, I've got to visit Mrs. Benford in forty-five minutes."

J.D. shook his head as he poured more coffee for both of them. "I can't be her anything. Let's make this short and sweet. Read my lips. *I'm not doing it.*" He put the coffeepot down and glared. "That's final. I've done my part." He sat down, reached for the paper and opened it to the sports page. The Rangers actually won a baseball game yesterday.

Meg glanced around the small kitchen. "Where's Kate?"

"Out collecting eggs. Schedule is working out just fine. She gathers the morning eggs while I have breakfast, then while I'm cleaning out the pens, she eats and then goes to work with the incubator in the hatching barn. We don't see each other till dinnertime." He mumbled the last word not wanting to remind himself of what happened at their evening meals.

Dinnertime was when Kate drifted around the kitchen like an angel and embroiled him in bewilderment. He found it impossible to keep his eyes off her shiny auburn hair swinging around her shoulders just begging to be touched. Each sway announced how it would caress his bare chest if they were close. Her hair wasn't the only attribute that caught his attention when the sun sent long shadows across the kitchen. He couldn't keep his gaze off her shapely breasts and legs. Even the quickest glance brought a tightening pulse to his loins.

But then his eyes would travel to her perfectly rounded abdomen and remind him she wasn't going to be at the Circle C forever. She was just staying for a while.

Meg broke into his thoughts with her stubbornness. ''I'm glad the situation is working out, but *nothing* is going to work out if I don't get her a coach. She has very little time to practice as it is. I figured since you two are living together, it would be easy to work together every night. Perfect opportunity. Just a few simple breathing exercises.'' She finished with a nod.

He sent her a deadly look over the edge of the newspaper. ''Wrong! We don't even see each other at night. After dinner, she goes in her room and does who knows what, and I watch a little TV and then I hit the sack.''

Shaking her head, Meg leafed through the Lamaze booklet. ''Well, then, you tell me who can be her coach, and I'll go convince them.''

''I'm not doing it.'' J.D.'s jaw set after he said the last word, but not before he noticed she'd set her jaw, too. Damn Meg. She *was* asking too much. He'd given in and let Kate stay, and the situation was working out better than he'd thought it would. She did save him a lot of time. But the Lamaze coaching—that was out of his league. He didn't need the intimacy of coaching to pull him closer to her.

His thoughts were doing it for him.

At night, the minute he fell asleep, Kate came dancing uninvited into his dreams with her sexy eyes, tempting mouth, lush breasts and sweet voice. He wound up exhausted by morning.

Meg's voice grew more serious. ''J.D., I wouldn't ask you to do this if it wasn't so important. I want Kate to have the baby naturally. It's better for both of them. You wouldn't want to be responsible—''

"Don't start with the guilt trip again," J.D. broke in with authority, his hand raised.

"It's not a guilt trip. You're the only one. The coaching isn't difficult, and I brought all the instructions you'll need. If you start tonight, you can get her ready before the baby comes. Lamaze is wonderful." She stopped long enough to point to the booklet. "Just thirty minutes of practice a day. You might find it interesting." She paused, leaned toward him and pulled the newspaper down to glare at him. "Are you listening to me?"

"Nope."

"Yes, you are. You like working with those weird ostriches, why not help Kate out?"

J.D. shook his head. "She not laying an egg, for heaven's sake! She's having a kid. And besides, maybe she doesn't want me for her trainer. Ever thought of that?"

Meg laughed gently. "Coach, not trainer. She's not trying out for the decathlon. As far as who helps, she doesn't have a choice. I'm scraping the bottom of the barrel with you."

"Thanks for the vote of confidence. I like the comparison."

"A very good barrel, though. When will she be back? I'd like to give her a checkup since I'm here. Save her a trip into town."

"'Bout six-thirty."

"So you'll do it?"

"Ah…Meg. I'm not good at stuff like this." Exasperated, he folded the paper again, picked up the pamphlet and thumbed through it. Sketches and words like "puffing" and "huffing" flashed up at him. Part of him wanted to help Kate, but helping meant getting involved. He'd let Meg railroad him one too many times already.

"Come on. You don't have to be in the delivery room, if that bothers you. Just coach her up until the hospital, then I'll take over from there. But for the life of me, I can't see you having a weak stomach. With all the procedures you have to do with those birds that look like something out of—"

J.D. held his hand up. "Not the same, Meg. They're birds not humans."

"If I didn't know you so well, I'd say you had a thing for Kate, and that's why you don't want to be her coach." Meg looked at him squarely.

"Wrong-o, Mego!" The idea was absurd. He liked his women unpregnant—and in no need of a coach for anything. Yeah, maybe he found her attractive, in a vague sort of sensual way. He assumed the seductive effect was a quirk. Nothing more than that.

Or was it?

He glanced at his cousin again. Her face held a knowing look he'd witnessed many times. Meg was seldom wrong. But today she was.

"Well, if you don't have anything at stake, why don't you help?" A smirk was growing on her face. She had him there. What difference did it make to him, anyway? Just to prove her wrong, he'd do it and forget his libido.

"Okay, for hell's sake, I'll do it just to get you off my back! Just to prove I don't have a *thing* for her." He stopped and took the booklet out of her hands. "What page do we start on?"

Smiling, she took the book back. "How come you're so sure Kate wants you to be her coach?"

Meg asked, her voice full of victory.

"Like you said, who else is there?"

"Scat!" Kate demanded, and pushed the home-made mop toward the bird. J.D. had invented the contraption when it was decided she'd collect the eggs. Anything taller than the ostriches scared them, and they'd run for cover.

"Scat, I've got work to do." The female ostrich scuttled toward her mate, kicking gravel and dust with large two-toed feet. Kate sighed. After talking to Meg this morning, she wasn't in a good mood. J.D. was to be her Lamaze coach, and the idea of him being so close *scared* her.

In the past few days she and J.D. had worked out a schedule where they didn't see each other that much. And she'd hoped it would help the hormone rampage a little. But the adage, "out of sight, out of mind" wasn't true. In fact, it seemed to work the opposite way. The more she didn't see him, the more she thought of him.

Meg had told her it was also common for her sense of smell to be enhanced—and it was true. His natural, heavenly aroma seemed to be all over the house, triggering more lustful feelings than she cared to acknowledge. And the nights were the worst.

Her dreams had grown into full-fledged festivals—colorful streaks of pleasure keeping her awake till the early morning hours. Every night in her dreams she melted into his big, hard body, pressed herself against his chest and made love to him.

She inhaled deeply and tiny jabs of delight ran through her body. The reaction only emphasized the fact she needed to stay as far away from J. D. Pruitt as was humanly possible.

With her newly collected eggs she walked down to the barn and slammed the door as she made her way into the barn to the incubator. It was time to do the afternoon check on eggs ready to hatch.

J.D. had shown her how to hold an incubated egg up to the light and outline the air sac. When there was only an inch left, she had to help the bird break through the tough eggshell. She liked helping the chicks hatch most of all.

She held an egg up to the light to check the progress. Taking a pencil, she drew a line dividing dark from light. She put the egg back in its holder. She picked up the small rubber mallet J.D. had shown her how to use, tapped lightly but firmly against the pencil line. The thick shell cracked unevenly along the tap line. She put the mallet down and pried the shell off. A white, rubbery membrane surrounded the tiny baby.

Kate gently pulled back nature's blanket. The wonder of creation and birth washed over her. A tiny chick folded inside the egg stared back, its large, glassy eye staring innocently up at her. "It's okay, tiny one, with some help and a few more hours, you'll have the strength to peck out."

She pulled the membrane carefully over the chick, placed the cap back and put the egg in a hatching position. The little bird would be out of the shell soon enough.

Her own baby kicked and wiggled against her. Kate laughed and pressed both hands to her belly. She patted the right side with a fingertip as if tapping on an egg.

Hopefully the Lamaze practice would be like someone tapping a shell and helping the baby out.

They were supposed to practice tonight. Kate steeled her thoughts. She knew a Lamaze partner had to work mighty close, and she didn't want J.D. within fifty feet of her.

She didn't think her heart could stand it.

"I can't do it anymore," Kate stated as she rolled onto her side, propped her hand under her chin and placed the other on her abdomen.

J.D. watched as Kate's hair shimmered magically around her shoulders. "But we haven't finished yet. The book says a half hour, no less. If we're gonna do it, we might as well do it right. We've still got stress management and guided imagery to get through."

He sat beside her, his legs folded tailor-style. Without thinking, he reached over and covered her hand. She slipped her hand from beneath his and placed her fingers on his wrist. Pulling his hand across to her belly, she pressed his palm against the taut skin. A tiny hiccup popped from inside and J.D. grimaced.

"What the hell was that? Everything okay?" he asked, making his voice steady, but he was more worried than he cared to admit.

"That's why I have to take a break. Somebody's got the hiccups." Kate pointed to her belly, then tried to smile, meeting his gaze. "It's pretty uncomfortable."

He lifted his hand from her stomach and brushed a tendril of hair from Kate's face. "You gonna be okay?" His fingers lingered on the silky strands, then traced the tiny curve of her ear as he tucked the strand behind it. Kate's stomach jumped again, and he dropped his hand to the swelling. It was another quick hiccup.

She laughed gently and then moaned. "It hurts a little, but it's funny." Her hand went to her stomach and grazed J.D.'s.

He was happy for a good excuse to stop the practice. He was so preoccupied with Kate, he'd been having trouble concentrating. Even if she was the prettiest woman he'd been around in a long time, and had the greatest smile he'd ever seen, he didn't need to be thinking about her so much. His promise to help was only to get Meg off his back, he reminded himself. But for the past twenty minutes, he'd been mesmerized by her.

In just the first few minutes he'd held her hand, rubbed her abdomen, encouraged her to breathe, softly and then fast and heavy. He was almost embarrassed that it reminded him of something far more personal than Kate practicing to have a baby.

Another hiccup popped, and they looked at each other and laughed. Kate moaned softly. "Oh-hh, this could go on for hours." Her face contorted with pain and made him feel he had to do something to help.

J.D. reorganized his legs, then helped Kate sit up. "I've got an idea." He crabbed around, positioning himself behind her. He stretched his legs down the length of hers, pulling her into the vee of his limbs.

"What is this? More Lamaze?" she asked, holding her abdomen.

He tugged her back against his chest. To his chagrin, she fit against him perfectly. "Partly. Maybe this will make you relax, and the little guy will, too." Pressing his hands to the base of her neck, he massaged the muscles from her skull out to her shoulders. "The book says this is a good way to ease tension." With the warmth from her body, he was more aware of his hands against her silky skin.

She made comfortable whimpering sounds as she relaxed into the massage.

"Another hiccup?"

"No. Your hands just feel so good. Sometimes my shoulders get cramped."

With her encouragement, he pressed a bit harder and worked at the tension within her flesh. He looked over her shoulder. The scoop-necked top she was wearing outlined her full, abundant breasts, and his fingers wandered to the slope of her shoulders where the succulent rise began. He would love to touch the full mounds.

The baby hiccupped again, and Kate's hands moved over her tummy. He wrenched his thoughts into line. "You said this happened before?"

"Once. I spent all night trying to get rid of them, but it didn't work." Her hands circled over her belly.

J.D. carefully rested his chin on her head and continued his massage. He could smell her hair, and it reminded him of lilacs—feminine and beautiful— like her. "You all by yourself when it happened?" He tried to stop himself from asking the question but couldn't.

"Uh-huh. Well, just me and the baby," Kate answered.

He pulled back a little. "Your ex-husband not there?" The thought of her being alone and needing someone angered him.

"We split up a month after I became pregnant." She tried to glance up at him. "But it was over before that. There are times when, even though it might be nice to have someone around, it's better to be alone.''

J.D. knew that feeling well. "You aren't afraid to have the baby by yourself?"

"I was at first, but not anymore. I trust Meg and…and you."

The last word ripped through him. He didn't want her trusting him. *"'I don't know nuthin' 'bout birthin' no babies, Miz Scarlett.'"* His voice came out sounding like Prissy in drag from *Gone with the Wind,* and she giggled. Even though he was kidding around, he wanted to discourage her from counting on him.

"You don't need to. I'm sure Meg knows her stuff." Her abdomen bounced again. "Oh-hh…oh-hh, that was a big one."

"I'd think the baby's father would want to be there." His statement was more direct than he wanted it to be. How could a man leave her and the baby?

"He's not interested. Remarried right after our divorce was final. He's got a new life and doesn't want anything to do with us." She stared at her belly.

J.D. didn't try to stop the two-word expletive that jetted out of his mouth. "Sorry, but it's gotta make you mad."

"It does, but I'm very capable of doing all this by myself."

His hands worked harder to relieve the stress in her shoulders. "How's that?"

"It feels wonderful."

"We could practice the imagery if you want," J.D. suggested, hoping to take his mind off Kate being so close. He could feel the heat from their bodies mixing.

"What are we supposed to do?" she asked softly. Her voice, like creamy red velvet, rubbed against him.

He swallowed trying to wet his now-dry mouth. "Think...think about relaxing. Pretend you're floating on water. Drifting on a raft and the sun's nice and warm and it's calm."

Kate nestled closer, causing pure radiance to flash through him.

"Ocean or lake?" she asked dreamily.

"Ah...lake, big one, just outside of San Antonio. Birds are singing, gentle waves lapping against the raft...." His fingers were still kneading her shoulders, and he forced himself not to press the rest of his body against hers.

She joined in. "We have our bathing suits on, and we're slathered in suntan lotion that smells just like coconuts." Her sweet, easy voice brought him into the image.

J.D. created a fine picture in his mind of Kate in a small bikini, her breasts as lush and perfectly formed as they were now, her stomach back to its naturally flat state, her hips curved into the small, cloth triangle that covered one strategic place.

Her voice softened even more. "Wouldn't that be wonderful? We could jump in the water anytime we wanted."

The strong impression made him speechless. He and Kate swimming, touching, kissing. All he wanted to do was pull her closer and bury his face in her hair. Inhale her sweetness and become a part of her.

She sighed deeply and her chest and belly heaved.

Knowing his dream was impossible, he forced himself to speak, breaking the seductive spell. "No more hiccups?"

His method of spell-breaking worked. She slipped from his hands and knelt in front of him.

"I think he or she is recovered," she answered. "I feel much better now." Her chest heaved and then she pulled herself to a full sitting position.

J.D. had come to admire her, and that's why he'd wanted to help her—to make the pain go away. But the knowledge made his gut ache and his mouth dry. Wanting to take her in his arms again and draw them into another imaginary journey, wasn't something he was used to feeling. He didn't dare do it again. The closeness was just too dangerous.

He was in one hell of a precarious position.

Wanting a woman like Kate was just plain crazy. Yet he couldn't deny the frigid, fiery feeling that sat just below his belly.

6

Kate savored the flavors of her Dairy Queen Super Burger. The two-inch sandwich was the only thing she missed about the city.

"Think you bought everything you need for the baby?" Meg asked.

With her mouth full, she nodded. She had quickly accepted Meg's invitation to drive to Fort Worth to purchase a layette for two reasons. First, to put a physical distance between J.D and herself, and second, she needed to get things ready for the arrival of her child. "Got everything on my list. Except I think the T-shirts I bought are too small."

Meg resettled herself in the red plastic chair and laughed. "Babies usually come out pretty tiny."

"The salesperson told me to buy the newborn size." Kate glanced down at her stomach and then back up at Meg. "But it doesn't look so little, does it? Every time I walk by someone, I'm afraid they're going to yell, 'Free Willy.'"

Gazing at her stomach, Kate laughed again, then sighed. It felt good to be away from J.D. and the Circle C, at least for a while. They'd been practicing Lamaze every night and the closeness was wearing on her nerves. The practice sessions had created a

thread of sensual light between them that could not
be denied or broken. And it caused Kate to be more
aware than ever of his appeal. Each day the overwhelming allure of her partner grew in exponential
proportions.

Every Lamaze session was sweet torture, sending
sensations trumpeting through her body she didn't
care to feel for any man, J.D. included. She'd vowed
any attachments would be reserved for her child.
Others, she could do without. Her terrible marriage
had caused enough trouble.

"If you think of anything else you need for the
baby, we can stop on the way out of town. We have
plenty of time. I scheduled the entire afternoon off,"
Meg announced between bites of her barbecue sandwich. "I almost forgot how much I like these darned
things."

"I wish I were an old hand at this instead of a
nervous new mother." Kate stopped and took a sip
of her soft drink.

"Don't worry. You'll be fine. If you need anything
else, I can always come back, or we can send J.D.
out on a few errands."

"I don't think J.D. wants to run errands for me."
Kate pressed her lips together, hoping she hid any
trace of the emotions sprinting through her body with
just the mention of his name. She still hadn't recovered from the fact she'd confided to Meg that she
was attracted to him. "By the time the baby's born,
he'll probably have found a place for us to move. I
know he wants me off the ranch." He hadn't said
anything lately, but Kate could ascertain how he
thought by his actions. How he avoided her. How he
kept his conversation about anything personal to a

bare minimum. Unfortunately for him, she hadn't changed her mind, either. She'd grown to love the Circle C Ranch.

Meg put her sandwich down and picked up her drink. "I know my cousin comes across as a hardhead, but he's really not. Most of it's just an act."

"He should get an Academy Award 'cause he fooled me."

"Believe it or not, he used to be a lot of fun. We did some crazy things together before Ann died. After that everything changed," Meg said with melancholy.

"Ann was his wife?" Kate remembered the name. She'd wanted to know more about her, but anytime her conversation approached the subject, J.D. bristled and either stopped talking or left the room. That part of his life was something he'd hidden away and didn't want to have dug up. Meg's cousin had buried his passions like a junkyard dog concealing treasures, and wasn't going to allow anyone to get near.

"They were married for five years. She was also my best friend. Still hasn't mentioned it to you?"

"Never says a word."

Meg shook her head. "Ann was his high school sweetheart. J.D. wanted to get married right after graduation, but Ann wanted to go to college with me. He won out, and they started working the Circle C. That's when it was a cattle ranch his mother left him." Meg paused, and with her index finger, drew an invisible square on the Formica-topped table. "He's always been so responsible. Still believes he's accountable for the entire world."

"Responsible?" Kate asked, repeating the word, wanting to put all the pieces of J. D. Pruitt together, but damning any interest in the man she knew was better kept at a distance.

"More than responsible. He's never said anything, but I think he feels Ann's death was his fault. Thought if he would have encouraged her to go to college...." Meg's voice dropped off. The low ceiling fan hummed above them. "After Ann, he'd sold all the cattle and was about to move God-knows-where when your uncle Charlie came along. He brought J.D. back around."

Meg's words submerged in her thoughts. His actions made a little more sense to her now. "Uncle Charlie was good at helping people," Kate said. "When he found out what my ex was doing, he was there for me." She recalled all the times her uncle had stood by her, or made her laugh or made her see the funny side of life.

"Charlie did wonders for him. Gave him a sense of purpose." Meg smiled, tilted her head and reached for her barbecue sandwich again. "Don't give up on him, Kate."

"I don't intend to. I don't want to give up the Circle C. It means a lot to me."

J.D. gazed around the neat hatching room in amazement. Kate had caught up the extra work that had been left since Charlie passed away. He let out a long, low whistle. The lady was efficient.

Wandering out into the concentrated Texas sun, he squinted toward the ostrich pens. He needed to check on the bird who'd lost his mate a few weeks ago. The male ostrich had been acting strangely. This morning Kate had mentioned she hadn't taken one fertile egg from the nest in over three weeks.

Herman! That's what she'd insisted on calling the animal. The bird wasn't mating with his new consort. What had Kate named her? Jezabel. He chuckled. She claimed Herman needed a mate to peak his interest, and maybe a Jezabel could do it. The woman, although stubborn as all get-out, was enticing.

Watch it, Pruitt. Thoughts like that will only get you in trouble. J.D. gave himself a lecture about the woman who was attracting more and more of his attention. Why couldn't he just put her in the back of his mind where he kept every other thought he didn't want to think about?

It was the darned Lamaze practice! He laughed out loud.

That and ten thousand other things.

Sure, working every night with her was bringing them physically close together, but that's not all it did. The evenings made him see Kate in another light. She worked hard at what she set her mind to, and he admired that quality in anybody. The way she did her work around the ranch was the same, too. She never complained about getting up early or the work itself. No, in fact she seemed to enjoy her chores. And from what he'd observed today, she was doing a good job.

But the Lamaze thing was causing odd sensations in his gut at night before he went to bed. Just like the feelings he was experiencing right now—a burning commotion when he even dared to think of her.

In the past three weeks, he'd become used to having her around the ranch. She had a way of filling the house with special warmth and good humor she carried around like silver moonbeams. Even though they didn't see each other very often during the day, he knew she was there and it created a closeness.

Today she'd left with Meg to go to Fort Worth to shop for the baby.

And he missed her.

He felt lost without her. When she was around, her smiles lifted his spirits and washed him with joy as they passed on the path or in the house. The empty sensation he felt now caused him to realize something else. His fingers tingled with the thought. He wanted to touch her, fill his hands with her lovely hair and run his fingers through it. Lower his mouth to hers and kiss her until they were both so dizzy they had to sit down.

He squinted at the afternoon sun. She'd be back soon. He cleared his throat. His lurid thoughts were out of the question, but his physical self seemed to have no reservations.

Grimly he looked toward the pens and thought about the women he could call. Since Charlie left the earth, he hadn't had time for his personal life. But he still had some women's numbers. He shook his head. Easing the tension below his belt wasn't the answer. Calling some woman just for *that* seemed a little too planned—too clinical.

He let fly with a few choice cusswords, then tried to push all thoughts of Kate to a part of his mind that stored the emotions he didn't have time for. He walked to the pen where Herman and Jezabel were held and stopped outside the gate. The rooster stood twenty feet away from the new female. J.D. didn't need to enter the pen. The nest wouldn't have a fertile egg. Kate had named the bird correctly—he was still a confirmed bachelor.

Herman was costing him plenty of money by eating his weight in feed and not doing his part to produce fruitful eggs.

Jezabel ruffled her feathers and squatted to draw the male's attention. "Get over there, you dumb bird," J.D. yelled as he threaded his fingers through the chain link and leaned forward, glaring past the open metal squares. "Don't you know a good female when you see her?"

Herman swung his neck, bellowed, turned and headed to the opposite end of the pen.

The late afternoon Texas sky boiled and bubbled with moist black clouds. J.D. glanced out the front window. He'd been exposed to Texas weather long enough to know bad news was blowing in from the west. "Unpredictable" described Texas climate at best. During spring and summer, a thunderstorm could churn up within minutes and raise a bushel of trouble.

"Is a storm coming?" Kate asked as she came out of her room.

J.D.'s gaze left the window and fell on her. She and Meg had come back from shopping half an hour ago, carrying in more bags than he could count. Their return eased the worried tension he'd been feeling about Kate making it home before the storm struck.

He nodded. "It's moving in fast. Lucky I collected the eggs. The weatherman says it's going to be a bad one." J.D. walked over, turned down the volume on the TV and sat on the couch.

"How about the ostriches? Do we need to do something?" Kate joined him. She smelled of fresh air, violets and sweetness, and the familiar pulsing started low in his belly.

J.D. stood and paced across the living room floor. "Nah, they'll be all right. Believe it or not, they *are* smart enough to get out of the rain. When it starts, they race under their sheds and stay until it blows over. Haven't had one hurt in a storm yet." He stopped his pacing long enough to look down at her.

She sat on the couch looking up at him, her face without makeup, her hair freshly shampooed and held in a ponytail at her neck. He fought the overwhelming need to be close to her. "Only thing I should do is get the chicks under cover just in case there's hail."

Kate pushed herself up and stood. "I'll help."

J.D. noticed her growing abdomen for the first time this afternoon. He didn't want her outside. "Stay here. I'll take care of the chicks. You must be tired. If I know Meg, she ran you around Fort Worth like a guided missile, shopping like crazy."

"I'm fine. I have a little backache, that's all. Guess I walked too much. I need to see how you get the chicks in the hatching barn." Kate kept in step with him as they walked through the house and out the back door.

Moist, heavy wind whipped around them as they tromped down the path. The rain hadn't started yet, but as J.D. looked up at the gorged dark sky, he reasoned it could be any minute, and he wasn't comfortable with Kate exposed to it. "Not much to getting the chicks to safety. Move their fence back into the hatching barn. I can handle it. Go on back to the house."

"I know you can handle it, but I need to know

just in case I have to do it myself sometime.'' Kate
smiled up at him, and he felt his stomach twist again.
He wouldn't be able to talk her into going back to
the house, so he needed to move fast.

He slowed his pace, remembering she'd mentioned
her back hurt. A loud whack of thunder rolled across
the area as they entered the yard in front of the hatching barn. Twenty chicks, three days old, squawked
and scratched the dirt. The newborns with fuzzy
heads were fenced in by two-foot high chicken wire
brought around in a circle.

J.D. lifted the padlock off the large barn doors and
swung them open. ''Need to inch the fencing up into
the barn,'' he yelled against the burst of sweeping
wind. ''Gotta get the water and feed inside the barn
first.''

Kate stepped over the fence and picked up the
feed. A grimace covered her face, and he noticed her
pursed lips. She moved into the barn with containers
and then came out, tendrils of auburn hair whipping
around her face. ''What now?''

Thunder crashed around them and small droplets
of rain began to fall. The storm was springing on top
of them. There'd be just enough time to get the
chicks under cover and get back to the house. ''You
okay?'' he asked grimly. For the first time Kate
looked tired, overly pregnant, and he worried about
her.

''I'm fine. Let's get going.''

''Okay, stand at the opposite end.'' J.D. put Kate
closest to the barn. ''We need to scoot the fencing
up into the barn, and the chicks will come right
along,'' J.D. hollered but was drowned out by the
thunder. He pantomimed what he wanted her to do.

If offer card is missing write to: Silhouette Reader Service, 3010 Walden Ave., P.O. Box 1867, Buffalo, NY 14240-1867

BUSINESS REPLY MAIL
FIRST-CLASS MAIL   PERMIT NO. 717   BUFFALO, NY

POSTAGE WILL BE PAID BY ADDRESSEE

SILHOUETTE READER SERVICE
3010 WALDEN AVE
PO BOX 1867
BUFFALO NY 14240-9952

NO POSTAGE
NECESSARY
IF MAILED
IN THE
UNITED STATES

Three minutes later J.D. stood with Kate in the hatching barn, both of them drenched with rain. "Chicks are soaked. Gotta set up heat lamps and close the doors," J.D. said, his glance trailing out to the storm. "The rain seems to be letting up a bit, you head on up to the house." He placed a hand on Kate's shoulder. To his surprise she was trembling. "Damn, you're freezing." He turned and marched into the office and brought out a large towel.

"I'm all right." Kate's voice quivered as she spoke. "The rain—"

"Quit being so stubborn." J.D. wrapped the terry cloth around her shoulders, then pulled the end up and rubbed the strands of her wet hair. "Go sit down and rest, and I'll set up the lamps. Should put you under one. With your hair like that, you look like one of the chicks."

Kate's hand immediately flew to her hair, and she patted it down. "I'm fine, really. The towel helps."

J.D.'s hand captured hers, and he rubbed it between his palms. The connection caused a tingling in the pit of his stomach, and he cursed softly. He didn't need to be thinking about how much she enticed him now. Bringing her out to the barn had put her in jeopardy. "Don't worry about your hair. Go sit and I'll get these little guys settled. Then we'll get back to the house." The cacophony of the chicks, wind and thunder encircled them.

After he'd set up the heat lamps, J.D. came back to her. "Want to try and make it back to the house?" he asked. His concern hadn't lessened.

Kate stood and grimaced. Her hands rested on her hips and her fingers massaged her back.

"Back still hurt?" His question came out raggedly.

She nodded, not saying a word. Her silence raised a chilling feeling in his gut. She usually either kidded him or argued. Her face had paled, her cheeks drained of any color.

She needed to be in the house where it was warm and she could lie down.

If anything happens to… He forced himself to stop the thought. Instantly he cradled her into his arms, and lumbered out the door, through the rain, up the path to the house. Large drops of rain battered them, and he trudged faster, pulling her closer, working to shield her. A snap of lighting cracked across the sky above them and three seconds later a clap of thunder reverberated through both of them. "Damn, that was close," J.D. growled through the pandemonium as he kicked open the door and carried Kate inside.

Reaching the living room, he placed her on the couch. "You okay? Not like you to let me carry you without some kind of argument." He tried to sound casual, but alarm filled him. Her face had turned as pale as skim milk.

"My back hurts. It started this morning and I thought I was just tired, but now I'm not so sure. I think it's back labor." Her voice sounded faint and little-girl-like.

"Better call Meg." Thunder punctuated his statement. He grabbed the phone, listened for a dial tone then slammed it down. "Damned thing is out. Let's get to the hospital." Sharp pounding against the roof brought both their gazes to the ceiling.

"Hailstorm," Kate announced with a tremble. "We can't leave. I heard golf-ball-size hail is expected. Last time a hailstorm hit it broke every window in my car.'' A grimace distorted her face as pain grabbed at her.

He picked up the phone again, listened, and slammed it back in the cradle. Looking directly at Kate, tightness expanded across his chest. Trying to break his own tension, he joked, ''Is this where I go in the kitchen and boil water?''

Kate smiled despite the cramping. ''The boiling water thing is just to keep the man busy. I can't imagine what anyone would use it for. Hot tea, maybe? I've read about back labor. Sometimes new moms are fooled. Now I know why.'' Her pains were coming regularly since she'd helped move the chicks. Another labor pain dipped to the deepest part of her back and started wrapping around her lower abdomen.

''Another pain?'' J.D. asked, then paced to the other side of the room and then back to the couch. ''Forget I asked that. Of course it's a pain.'' Again he paced. Kate had never seen him so nervous. ''What we need to do is think,'' he stated dramatically.

''J.D.—''

''We need to devise a plan on getting you to Meg, or getting Meg over here. I can't possibly—''

''J.D.—''

He turned and walked back to the couch. ''We could try to drive over to Meg's—''

''J.D., I think my water just broke.'' Kate interrupted his anxious monologue with a complete thought. The thumping on the roof accented her words. ''I don't think we're going anywhere while it's hailing.'' She was touched by his nervousness as she counted her breaths and checked the clock on the far wall.

"Staying here isn't such a good idea." His pacing began again.

"I need to get out of these wet clothes," she murmured. As she stood, water dripped down her legs. "I'll be right back." She headed toward her room, excited yet nervous. Her pains were coming faster now, and by timing the last three, she knew she didn't have much longer. J.D. would have to help her.

After changing into a dry nightgown, she sat on the edge of the bed and breathed deeply, forcing herself to remain calm. Hail pummeled the roof. The sheer force of another pain caused her to lean back into her pillow. She closed her eyes and she heard herself groan.

"Hey! You all right in there?" J.D. yelled from the living room.

"Not really. I think you'd better come in here." Her voice sounded strange and detached to her own ears.

He marched to the doorway and leaned in. "I finally got through to Meg. She doesn't want you to risk going out. Said she'll be right over."

"Thank goodness," Kate murmured, breathless from the last labor pain. She sat up again.

"Why are you lying down?" More nervousness etched his brow.

The insane remark brought a chuckle to her lips through the aching she felt. "Having a baby." She said the words as casually as she could manage through her fear, anguish and exhilaration.

"Now?" Beads of perspiration glistened on J.D.'s forehead in the artificial light.

Nodding, she waited for a labor pain to subside. J. D. Pruitt wasn't the type of man to fear anything, but he sure looked intimidated at the moment. "My labor pains are close together and I feel different." A pain rolled up her spine and gripped around her abdomen. "Oh...this one is strong," she whispered, and closed her eyes, hoping to ease the discomfort.

When she opened her eyes, a look of sheer determination had taken the place of nervousness on his face. He closed the small space between them and sat next to her on the edge of the bed.

"It's rough outside," he said, looking down at his feet.

"Think everything'll be all right?" Kate grabbed his arm as a pain started to engulf her world again.

He turned and put his hands on her shoulders and spoke quietly. "Kate, take slow, even breaths... remember how we practiced?" He stroked her bare arms and spoke softly to her. "Cleansing breaths...smooth and even...you're doing great."

She worked to breathe the way he directed her to do. It felt so good to have him beside her, concerned and caring. She'd convinced herself for so many months she didn't need anyone, yet now his words and touch soothed and allowed her to be vulnerable. "I'm not sure I can do this, J.D."

As if sensing she needed him, J.D slipped closer to her, his arm sliding around her shoulders, holding her. "You can. We'll get through this together," he whispered against her cheek. "Meg will be here soon and I'll help you. Are you tired?"

His words calmed her. "I don't think I could collect any ostrich eggs right now."

"Not ready to conquer the world by yourself?"

She shook her head and rubbed her fingers against the smooth fabric of his shirt. "Maybe a very small world. I'm scared."

"Don't be scared, baby. You'll do just fine. That's why we did all the practicing," he said, still holding her.

"Do you think Meg can get here without getting hurt? I'd feel terrible if something happened to her." Her voice dropped to a whisper. The closeness and tension spiraled them into their own sphere—sealed together through sheer need.

"Yeah, if I know Meg, she'll be just fine. The hail's let up a little," he murmured against the top of her head. "Why don't you lay down? You'll feel better." He stood, but didn't move from the edge of the bed.

Taking his advice, she brought her feet up and lay back on the pillow. She wanted J.D. to be with her the entire time, but she hadn't forgotten what he'd said. He'd help but only up to delivery. "I hope I can remember everything we practiced."

He sat beside her again, his hands on her shoulders. "Don't worry. It'll work out."

Another pain surged up the small of her back tying itself around her. She groaned and then puffed.

"Kate, go with it, don't fight the pain. Remember what we did. Think good thoughts. Breath deeply...easy now...slow." His fingers massaged her shoulders as he encouraged her.

She felt beads of perspiration forming on her forehead as the pain receded. Wrapping her fingers around his arms, she sighed. Her contractions were stronger and closer together. Thankfully she heard Meg's voice.

"Hey, I'm here. For a minute I didn't think I was going to make it. Heck, the hail is as big as golf balls. My windshield's broken all to—'' Meg walked into Kate's room, her fingers combing wet strands out of her face. "How close are your contractions?"

"Two—three minutes apart," J.D. announced, then stood. "They're pretty strong. We've been using our Lamaze."

"Good. This is the time you both practiced for. Kate, we can't make a run for the hospital. All the roads are flooded. I checked the weather station and it's even worse south of here.'' Meg glanced at J.D. "Don't take this the wrong way, but you're all wet, Mr. Pruitt."

J.D. glanced down at his clothes. "I need to change. Will you stay with her?" he asked, the agitation back in his voice.

Meg laughed. "That's what I'm here for. Take it easy. Go get some dry clothes on and then get in here. We've got some work to do."

He rushed from the room, but not before glancing back at Kate. "I'll be right back."

Meg sat on the bed and held her hand. "We'll have to deliver the baby here. Are you okay with that?"

Kate wiped the back of her free hand across her forehead, wet her lips and groaned. "Do I have a choice? Oh, God, it's another one. They're getting stronger."

Meg placed her hand on Kate's tight abdomen. "It's okay, Kate, it won't be long now. Go with the pain…don't fight it…breathe deeply." They worked through the pain together.

J.D. walked into the room in dry clothes. "Everything all right?"

"Fine, she's a trooper. Doing just great," Meg answered, checking her watch.

Kate moaned again. "Here comes another one."

J.D. stepped to the other side of the bed and leaned closer, taking Kate's hands, looking straight into her eyes. "Come on, baby, you can do it. Breathe with me—like we practiced." He rubbed her hands gently.

His warmth soothed her and eased the pain somewhat.

"Breathe…long…and slow…that's it. You're doing great."

As Meg readied the room for the birth, Kate's contractions became stronger and closer together. J.D. encouraged her as Kate worked to control the pain, aware of J.D.'s help, concern and patience.

During each contraction he helped her measure her breathing, and after, he wiped her forehead with a cool washcloth.

I'm so tired," she groaned after a rush of contractions. "I can't do it." She squeezed one of his hands as he stroked her forehead with callused fingers.

"Yes, you can. We'll do it together. Won't be long now."

Meg came to stand by the bed. "You're doing a great job, both of you. I've been timing the contractions and you're almost ready." Meg moved to the end of the bed. "We need to get you down here. Can you help her, J.D.?" They worked together to scoot Kate where Meg wanted her.

"Are you ready to push?" Meg asked, and Kate nodded. "Good, with the next contraction, lean forward and grab your knees. J.D. steady her back. Okay, take a deep breath, let it out, and then hold the next."

Kate groaned and squeezed her eyes closed. One minute she felt like she could run a marathon, the next like a wet dishrag. On the next contraction she pushed as J.D. encouraged her.

"That's great, Kate. Now on the next contraction push with all your might. J.D. support her back," Meg demanded, and smiled at her patient. "You're doing quite a job. So's he."

"If I don't pass out, I'll be all right. Better give me my grade later, Doc." J.D. pressed his strong hands against her back.

"Here it comes," Kate groaned.

"Come on, push, baby. You're wonderful, Kate, wonderful," J.D. chanted.

Meg smiled a huge grin. "The baby's head's crowning. Push hard. You're about to meet your child."

7

$$\longrightarrow \longleftarrow$$

Totally amazed and awestruck at what had taken place at the Circle C, J.D. continued to stare out the kitchen window. Fragments of orange and pink glass-like colors filtered and shifted through the dark, broken clouds and scattered a rainbow across the horizon.

His cousin's voice broke into his thoughts. "For a person who didn't want to get involved, you certainly did a great job," Meg announced as she poured coffee into a mug.

Turning, he glanced across the kitchen, feeling a grin growing on his face. "Did a good job, didn't we?" Now able to shed the worry, pride welled inside him at the thought of helping Kate through the birth.

"I'd say. That's a beautiful baby in there." Meg nodded, then stirred her coffee, steam feathering up around her fingers. "I'm not sure Kate would have done as well if you hadn't been around. Your encouragement helped her through labor." She walked to him and patted his shoulder.

"Maybe, maybe not." He shrugged, not able to reconcile the new connection he had with Kate.

"What's next? We need to take them to the hospital?"

"No. Kate's fine and that handsome son of hers is healthy. If I check them into the hospital, they'll be isolated, and I don't want that. But the baby needs to be seen by a pediatrician. I've got a friend in Fort Worth who'll come out to the house and check him. Kate just needs to rest for a while."

"She was amazing, wasn't she? I don't think I've ever seen a woman act as strong and controlled as she did. Pretty cool the entire time." He shifted his gaze to the window again, hoping it would stop the pride from growing in his chest. It didn't work, and he turned to Meg. "Kate's the most unbelievable woman I've ever met," he added.

"You were pretty amazing, too. I don't think I've witnessed a man so calm in a long time." His cousin took a sip of hot coffee.

J.D. shook his head. "All an act. I was nervous as hell. That comment about passing out was no joke. I felt pretty dizzy at one point." His composure during the entire episode surprised him.

"That's normal. "Why don't you go in and see her? I need a break. Think I'll just sit here and drink my coffee for a while." She patted the table and sat down.

"Think it's okay?" His heart was pounding against his chest. "I've done a lot of egg cracking around the ranch, but today…" he said, and then exhaled. "Well, seeing a human being born is a whole other ball game. When that little guy looked at me…felt like a miracle…." He couldn't continue, his throat was so tight.

"Sure is," Meg murmured as he turned to go see his houseguests.

"Are you all right?" Kate smiled weakly at J.D. then gazed at her child she held in her arms. The newborn was a perfect vision.

"I'm fine. You're the one we should be worried about. Now I know why my mama used to compare having a baby to pushing a football out your nose." J.D. stepped to the side of her bed and gazed down at them. "Darn hard work."

Kate ran a fingertip down the infant's tiny turned-up nose. His skin was softer than she could have ever imagined. "I'm all right, tired though. Isn't he beautiful?"

"More than beautiful, maybe magnificent," J.D. answered, his voice gruff and thick. "Meg says that you're both healthy."

Kate gazed at the man who'd help her get through it all. "J.D., you were wonderful. I didn't think you'd stay through the entire delivery, but you did." She brought the baby up to her lips and kissed his ruddy cheek.

"Figured I might as well stick around." He sat carefully on the edge of the bed and stared at them. "He looks kind of scrawny."

"Oh, he won't be for long. When he's two he'll be running through the house like a Sumo wrestler."

J.D. reached out and touched the baby's hand.

"Charlie, meet J.D., J.D. this is Charlie."

"Charlie, huh?"

"After my uncle."

J.D. nodded and swallowed hard. "Charlie would have liked that. And a middle name?"

"I was thinking about James Dean. After you. Charlie James Dean Owens. If that's all right?"

J.D. swallowed again and cleared his throat. He blinked his eyes at Charlie. "It does have a strong ring to it." He reached across and rubbed the baby's fist. "Nice to meet you, little guy." Charlie's fingers unfurled, and J.D.'s finger filled his tiny hand.

"Look at that. The little guy already has a grip like steel." J.D. pulled his finger up and down.

Kate's heart beat faster. She'd wondered how J.D. would respond to her son.

J.D.'s face softened more. "Hey, there. You must be one tired little buckaroo," J.D. tried to coo. As if on command Charlie yawned. "He yawned!"

"Of course, he can do it all. Yawn, cry, blink his eyes." She laughed with gentleness. J.D. had never been around newborns, and his innocence was intoxicating. "He can manage all the bodily functions. Wait and see."

"Like two o'clock feedings and diapers?"

"Uh-huh. Want to hold him?"

"Nah, I might hurt him."

"Don't be silly. Just put your arms like a cradle and make sure you support his head and neck." Before he could protest she handed the baby to him. J.D.'s back was stiff as a board as Charlie snuggled in his arms.

"What neck? I don't see one."

"He's pretty much of a neckless wonder." Kate peered at her son.

"Am I doing it right?"

"Yes. It's hard to hold a baby wrong." She leaned back against the pillows, looked at the two males in front of her and sighed. Charlie looked a lot like her ex and that tore her heart out. But he had her eyes.

Her gaze shifted to J.D. The look on his face was one of sheer delight. Like the proud papa. Kate drifted back to the baby. She couldn't let herself think *that* thought for one moment.

J.D. slogged down the muddy path to the pens and noted the damage from the hailstorm seemed minimal. Reaching Herman and Jezabel's pen, he opened the gate.

"You birds okay?" he yelled the rhetorical question.

The ostriches stood close together under the corrugated awning that protected them from storms and cold. With large glossy eyes and craning necks, both birds stared at J.D.

"Finally making friends?" he asked. It was the first time he'd seen the pair close to each other. As he approached the animals, Jezabel took long-legged steps out to the open area of the pen, but the male stayed under the covering. "Starting to like her, are you?" J.D. yelled as he checked their food supply. The male bird shifted his neck and stared at his owner fearfully. Then the six-foot ostrich scurried toward his partner.

J.D. yawned. Although tired, he doubted if he could sleep. Every time he closed his eyes he saw Kate and Charlie. Even after struggling through labor and birth, she was still the most beautiful woman he'd ever seen.

He'd spent the past few weeks fighting a growing need for Kate. This afternoon he'd allowed himself the luxury to acknowledge his feelings. And those emotions were filling in places he'd forgotten were empty.

There were certainly no words to describe the way he felt when he saw her son and her response to him. She and Charlie had needed him today, and he wanted to protect them both. He opened the pen gate and stepped out and closed it behind him. Leaning against the fence, his gaze shifted to the cloudy sky. A slow, sinking feeling lodged in his gut and grew to deeper proportions. He had wanted to protect Ann, too.

The cool spring breezes warmed and stirred as part of April and all of May melted into the blistering heat of June. Hordes of Texas wildflowers bloomed against the blue-green field grass, and the days grew longer and the nights sultry.

Kate picked Charlie up from his crib that crowded her bedroom. In six weeks her child had flourished, becoming an alert, roly-poly happy baby. "Ready to go out to the hatching barn, darling?"

She brushed her fingers under his rounded chin, and he formed his mouth into a tiny circle. "You like the barn, don't you? Well, come on."

Out on the porch she placed him in his stroller and bumped it gently down the steps.

As she and Charlie strolled down the path to the barn, she saw J.D. Leaning the rake against the fence, he unbuttoned his plaid cotton shirt, took it off and hung it on the fence. Then he stretched in the late afternoon sun. His chest glistened, the sheen magnifying the muscles carving his upper torso.

Kate groaned, but kept on walking, her gaze never leaving him. Keeping her desire under control was proving to be a difficult chore. More difficult than she could have imagined. She thought when her pregnancy ended, the sexual yearnings would terminate, but they were only enhanced. Every day she used most of her energy to push back the urgent need for her partner.

"Hey," was all she had the strength for when she reached him.

"Gonna count eggs?" He pulled a blood-red kerchief out of his jeans' pocket.

Her gaze was still trained on him as he wiped the bright material across his brow, his bronzed skin stretching across his well-defined shoulders.

"Yes. The humidity levels in the incubator have been acting funny. I thought I'd check them." She swallowed hard. Every day it was becoming more difficult to keep her distance from him. And being in such close proximity, but unable to touch him, created deep, compelling needs. Yet she fought them with all her heart.

"How's the little guy?" He nodded to the stroller.

"He'll be hungry in a while." Kate stepped around to the side of the blue and white striped awning and pulled it back. Charlie squirmed and tongued his pacifier out, his face puckering like an old man's.

"Looks like he's getting ready to blow," J.D. said as he came around the stroller to stand beside her. His familiar way with Charlie reminded her how far they'd come in six weeks.

They'd gone back to their routine after Charlie's birth and the weeks had flown. The only thing that wasn't the same was the way they were with one another. Now there was a strong connection that felt like a family bond.

To make matters more difficult, J.D. was enthralled with everything Charlie did and his interest quickly grew into love. She could see it in his gaze every time he looked at her child. His response surprised her. She'd expected him to be grumpy with Charlie.

Early on, J.D. insisted on getting up with the baby for his late night feedings so she could get some sleep. All her arguing wouldn't convince him of anything else. One night, unable to sleep, she decided to get a glass of milk and before she'd reached the living room, she stood immobile in the hallway listening to J.D. talking to her child in a husky whisper. She took the liberty of eavesdropping, unable to move at the sound of J.D.'s one-sided conversation.

J.D. advised her son how he must be good to his mother, treat her right and take care of her. Then his voice dropped lower, and he kissed the top of Charlie's fuzzy head. He went on to tell him how he expected him to go to college, make him proud and be an honorable and honest person.

The concrete vision of the three of them moving through the years together seared her thoughts and made her eyes water. She had crept back to bed with a lump in her throat.

"He's been fussy all day. Probably getting tired of my face," Kate said after swallowing hard at the memory.

J.D. swooped down and brought Charlie out of his stroller. Holding him up in the air, his arms straight, he grinned up at the child. "Better treat your mama right, little guy." Charlie laughed a toothless grin. "That's right, laugh at J.D." He brought him to nestle in his arms and chucked him under the chin.

"Want to come with me up to the house? We'll both have some refreshments." The baby cooed at his well-known voice, and J.D. laughed out loud. "He's not fussy. Just needed some man talk."

"I don't know how you do it, but you certainly have a way with him. You're spoiling him."

"Tell you what. Go on to the hatching barn, and I'll take Charlie up to the house. His formula in the fridge?"

She nodded.

"Good. Then you won't have to feed him when you're finished. Come on, Charlie, let's give your mama some space." J.D. set the baby back in the stroller and snatched his shirt from the fence.

Kate watched as he pushed the stroller back up the dusty path. Drawing in a breath, she steadied herself. They were becoming more and more like a family.

J.D. stood by the kitchen sink enjoying the dinner smells. The stove held steaming pots and pans, and delicious smells permeated the kitchen. He'd become used to the large, sumptuous meals she so easily prepared over the past few weeks. His gaze slipped around the compact room. She'd set the table, and the rest of the house was neat and clean, just the way she kept the hatching barn.

J.D. listened for Charlie's cry, but the house was quiet. The baby was darned good for a little guy. He held the baby bottle under the rush of water and chuckled thinking about how Charlie had guzzled down the formula a little while ago. The past weeks had been a real awakening about kids. *And himself.*

He thought the baby would get on his nerves, but the situation had wheeled around opposite to what

he thought. Holding Charlie actually relaxed him after a hard day. And when he gazed at Charlie in
Kate's arms, hell, his chest expanded—he felt like
he was going to explode with pride and hope.

"Hungry?" Kate asked good-naturedly as she
walked into the kitchen. Her hair shined and it swung
against her sweetly curved shoulders.

"Uh-huh," was all he could answer as his gaze
held hers. Her good looks amazed him. After only
six weeks her figure was back to normal and every
time he saw her, she took his breath away. Basically
she looked the same; her skin still glowed and her
eyes still took on the sexy gaze at times that tore into
his gut. But with the pregnancy over, something else
took control of him.

His gaze settled on her light blue shorts. They allowed him to drink in her other attributes. Her
shapely legs hadn't changed, no, they'd only gotten
better with the golden tan she was acquiring in the
Texas summer sun.

He followed the smooth line down to her feet.
She'd painted her nails a pastel peach that enhanced
the color of her skin. A deep desire ripped through
his loins, and his mouth went dry. With a concerted
effort he turned his attention upward and the swelling
below his belt buckle got even worse.

Her abdomen was flat and the soft indention of her
waist flared into gently rounded hips. His gaze pulled
up to the curve of her lush breasts that strained at
her bra and thin T-shirt. The faint outline of her nipples was apparent through the light peach material,
and his eyes narrowed on the hardened beads that
strained against it.

The denim forming his jeans had become distinctively less comfortable, and he forced himself to think of something else. "Have a good day?"

"Yes, I got a lot of work done. How 'bout you?" She busied herself at the stove, stirring one of the pots.

"Charlie doin' okay?" More than anything else he admired the way she was with Charlie.

She glanced up at him. "Thanks for feeding him. He's sleeping. He'll probably snooze through dinner. Ready to eat?" she asked, her voice as soft and smooth as the summer evening. "You said you're hungry."

J.D.'s mouth went dry. He turned to the sink for a drink of water. He was hungry, all right, but not for what was on the stove. Her flowery perfume wafted toward him as she came up to the sink to rinse a spoon.

"Excuse me," she whispered.

Her closeness pushed and jumbled all his rational thoughts to the back of his mind and buried them, letting his lustful ones jut out and take over any control he might have.

"J.D., are you ready to eat?" The repeated question plunged into his mind and brought him back to reality.

"Sure. What's on the stove?" He sniffed the air again, trying to calm his runaway energy.

"I made Oriental beef with rice and vegetables. Do you like Chinese?"

Turning, his gaze followed her as she stepped to the stove. "If it tastes as good as it smells...." His voice trailed off with the smooth sway of her hips. Her shorts just covered her well-rounded bottom, the hem accenting its firmness. His breath caught in his chest and forced out any other thoughts.

"I think you'll like it."

"Know I will..."

She turned to face him; her steady green-eyed stare, compounded with the sexy squint, sent a bolt of pure adulation to his heart and groin.

"Well, let's eat."

His gaze crossed the table as she drew the fork up to her lips. They were the color of the inside of a seashell and shaped like a delicate butterfly. He wondered what it would feel like to touch his lips to hers. To run his tongue around them and feel the warmth of her being.

Suddenly, as if wishing could make it so, her own tongue darted out across her bottom lip and sent a jolt to his chest.

Putting her fork down, she stared back at him. "Aren't you going to eat any more? It's very good if I say so myself." A tinkle of laughter escaped her lips. "J.D.?"

"Huh?"

"I thought you said you were hungry."

"I am."

"Why aren't you eating?" She waited for him to answer, a quizzical look crossing her brow.

"Sorry," was all he could say. He took another bite and nodded. "Good. Real good." Shaking his head, he tried to force the erotic thoughts to the back of his mind. There was no point in torturing himself.

"We had three more hatchlings this morning. This is the best week we've had so far," she announced. "I've got an order for six chicks to be sent to California and another two need to go to Oregon next week.'' A proud expression covered her face.

''You've done a good job.''

''Thank you.''

They ate in silence for a while, and when they finished, Kate stood to clear the table.

''I'll do the dishes. You cooked,'' J.D. announced, leaving his chair.

''No, it won't take a moment to do these.'' Picking up their plates and turning toward the sink, Kate crashed head-on into him.

''Hey,'' he rumbled, an arm wrapping around her, his free hand catching the unsteady dishes. J.D. perceived the grab of breath in Kate's chest and her reaction actually made him shaky. She didn't stiffen in his arms. No, it was almost the opposite.

''Sorry, I didn't mean to almost knock you down.'' Her words came out all in one breath, and she turned, placing the dishes on the table.

His hands didn't leave her shoulders, and he swung her back to face him.

Her eyes were wide, childlike. The green-gold flecks in them glimmered. But it was her half-open mouth that held him magically captivated. He wanted to kiss her and have her kiss him back, expand the passion and demand for the woman he held in his arms. He wanted to kiss her yet he knew it wasn't a good idea. Heck, she was leaving soon. No use starting something.

And if he kissed her? J.D. knew he wouldn't be able to stop. The woman standing in front of him had a power over him. The stark wisdom caused him to swallow hard.

With a gentle flick of her kitten-like tongue, she

wet her bottom lip. J.D. groaned, resounding and sensual. Her feminine essence captivated him, in spite of his oath to not get involved. An uncontrollable need for this woman whisked away all the dark feelings that vined around his heart and held him back. He didn't want to need Kate. And he remembered he'd made a vow to get her out of his life...for her sake. He pulled back, but her sexy stare brought him back.

He leaned toward her, his fingers lacing through her hair, bringing his mouth closer to hers. "Kate," was all he was capable of whispering.

A sudden piercing cry cut into the moment and the incredible woman in his arms stepped back.

"That's Charlie." Her words came out quickly. She pulled from his arms and was out of sight in a matter of seconds.

"Mama's little guy was hungry tonight," Kate cooed as she finished diapering her son. The open window next to the crib allowed the cool night air to float toward her, fanning her flaming skin. Her heart was still jumping from her encounter in the kitchen with J.D. The tingling in the pit of her stomach joined her thumping heart and caused torrid emotions.

"Come on, darlin', we need some fresh air." She picked him up. Maybe a good dose of night air would cool her passion. *If only I hadn't reacted to J.D.* The thought flamed her cheeks more.

But she had, and now the clash between passionate needs for the man she'd been sharing a house with, and violent urgency to get as far away from him as possible could not be denied. She sighed, holding Charlie close.

The duplicity of her thoughts ripped her in two.

"Oh, Charlie, your mama is such a fool. I'm not good at picking men. Only you, sweetie." She held the baby and studied his face. He smiled at her, his toothless grin making her laugh. "I know. You like him. I can tell when he holds you how much you enjoy it. I did, too, tonight. But I've got to stand alone. For you and for me." The baby gurgled and drew a fist up to his mouth.

Out in the living room she placed Charlie in his stroller that sat by the front door. Peeking in the kitchen, she noted J.D. had finished the dishes. He was probably in his room. Back at the front door she strolled Charlie onto the small wooden porch.

The dark evening reminded her of the night she'd arrived at the Circle C. She sat on the step and leaned back against the smooth porch railing and pushed the stroller gently back and forth against the worn boards. The pounding of her heart mixed with the night noises.

Another gentle breeze, a mix of wildflowers and rich, moist earth, lifted and stirred her hair off her neck. An image of J.D.'s mouth against her own weaved its way into her mind and a burning need reached up and shattered all her reason. She'd wanted to succumb to him, but Charlie's cry reminded her she didn't have room in her life for J.D.

Charlie whimpered, seemingly in response to her thoughts. She'd never trust her judgment again when it came to men. She brought the stroller close and rubbed Charlie's tummy. He cried harder and Kate sighed.

The front screen slammed, and the baby jerked slightly at the sharpness. Kate didn't dare turn. She could feel J.D.'s gaze on her. She sat very still, knowing if she moved at all, she'd tremble at the thought of being close to him again.

J.D. knelt by Charlie and put his finger next to his small hand. Charlie gripped it, and J.D., with his other hand, stroked the baby's forehead. "Hey, little guy, you're gonna be all right," he cooed, his rough voice descending to a masculine whisper. Soon Charlie calmed down and stopped his fussing. A yawn stretched his small mouth.

J.D. stroked his skin and the sleepy baby released his finger.

"You doing all right?" His voice was low.

Even a few words could set her soul on fire. "Uh-huh."

Gently moving the stroller out of the way, he sat beside her on the step, their thighs parallel, hips touching. She needed all her self-control to keep her hands pressed to her sides and not let them wander to him.

He tipped his chin up and gazed up at the sky, a blanket of tiny pinpoints of light. "Nice night. Look at those stars. Every time I come out here I'm amazed there's so many."

Kate's gaze followed his. A star-coated black velvet cover expanded over them. "Sometimes I wonder what's really up there. Maybe other earths, other universes like ours." She brought her voice to a whisper. "People just like us moving through life, wondering what it's all about." They were so close, his breathing ebbed and flowed against hers as his body heat mesmerized her.

He didn't say a word as his arms naturally swept around her, pulling her closer. He held her gently for a few heart-pounding moments, and then with his fingertips under her chin, he tipped her face up to meet his.

"Oh, God, Kate..." he murmured against her cheek as his mouth traveled to her burning lips. She felt the hard strength of his hands on her, his fingers reading her like braille. His mouth crushed against hers, and she willingly parted her lips to accept his searching tongue.

A thrill traveled through her from the soles of her feet to the top of her head. She couldn't think at all. Moaning lightly, Kate kissed him back, unable to contain the rush of pent-up emotion. Her hands played against him as pleasure surged and pulsed. Entranced by his taste and touch, she craved more of him.

He slipped a powerful hand under her T-shirt, splaying fingers against her flat middle. Kate's mind reeled with erotic sensations. The jolt of sexual need rocked her very core.

Her hand automatically traveled over his strong thigh, her fingers needing to touch him, caress him, to quench her growing passion.

Manly fingers searched against her fiery skin and found her breast. Gently he slipped her engorged orb from its lacy cup and played with the peaked bud. "Kate...." He groaned her name as his mouth sought the curve of her neck. His tongue flicked against her skin, and he moaned.

A pleasurable aching pulsed within her, and she sighed. Not being able to control herself, her fingers crept deliciously up his inner thigh to his hard manhood.

He crushed her to his chest as his mouth found hers again. "Kate, let's go inside," he urged.

The words conjured up a blockade inside her, and she pulled from him, her lips still tingling, drunk from his kisses. The dim living room light from the window highlighted the frustration in his face.

If I don't pull back now, I never will.

She had to stop herself from this madness. She'd been so easily led before, so disappointed. She'd promised herself over and over it would never happen again. She had Charlie to think about now. She had to worry about making a life for him. There was no room for anything else. Her child was more important than anything her body demanded from the man who held her in his arms.

With a sigh, she drew on her resolve. "I can't believe what we just let happen. This isn't a good idea," she said, working to rein in her erratic breathing.

"It's one hell of a great idea." He reached for her, but she forced herself to scoot away.

The move caused a look of hurt on his face. "Trying to tell me you didn't like it?"

"No!"

"Then why was it such a bad idea? You could tell I obviously enjoyed it."

Her eyes darted to the top of his thigh. Yes, he enjoyed the kiss. She cleared her throat. "Because we're partners. You and I have no business kissing each other. It won't work."

"It'll work, believe me." He glanced down at the

bulge in his jeans, and she knew exactly what he meant.

"I didn't mean that. We're business associates, not lovers. And I don't want to get involved—this way." She let her chin jut out, trying to show him she was serious. But within her heart there was a dichotomy. She wanted him, yet fear stopped her. "I have other things to worry about. My son, getting my life back on track and making a living. I don't have time or energy for this."

"Lady, you could have fooled me a minute ago."

"I'd appreciate it if you didn't make any more passes at me." She narrowed her eyes slightly, hoping she could convince him.

"I've never been one to force myself." His face fell as if he were digesting the thought.

"That's good. We don't need this problem." Her heartbeat kicked up a level.

"Funny, I don't look at it as a problem."

"Well, it is. It's best we stay away from each other," she said.

He gazed at her a moment, nodded and, without saying a word, stood and walked back into the house.

Kate stood and looked in the stroller. Charlie was sound asleep. She sat back down and pressed her back against the wooden railing and sighed, wishing her heart would stop pounding. The memory of J.D.'s lips against her own caused her to grow dizzy with need. But how could she go back on her promises she'd made to herself and her son? Keeping herself focused on her life with Charlie was the most important issue. Yes, she'd done the right thing by stopping. Thank goodness she'd had the strength to rein in her feelings.

Now all she had to do was keep the promise to herself.

J.D. shut his bedroom door quietly, leaned against the smooth wood and filled his lungs with much needed oxygen. His comfortable bedroom now felt cramped and stifling. The muscles in his upper arms and neck ached, and he rolled his shoulders to relieve the tension of having Kate ripped from his arms.

I've got to stop thinking about her.

He drew in another breath and realized she'd become a part of him. Kate's special scent, still clinging to his shirt, assaulted his reason with each burst of her fresh, lilac bouquet. He craved to have her back in his embrace, her delicate arms around his neck, her sweet, soft lips pressed to his, and her moist, hot tongue searching, needing, wanting—

He tried to shake the thought away. Grinding his back teeth, he fought the pounding in his groin. He had to stop thinking about her, or he'd head right back out to the porch and kiss her again.

The squeak of the screen door let him know Kate and Charlie had come inside.

He moved to the far side of his room and sat on the edge of his twin bed. Soon Kate would be in her own room, right next door, with only a wall keeping them apart.

J.D. gritted his teeth again and wondered how in the hell he was going to stay away from her. He unclenched his fingers and stared down at his left hand. His skin was dusky from working outside so much. Five years ago stark whiteness ribboned his left ring finger where his wedding band had been.

The pallid skin had served as a reminder—a beacon when he forgot.

J.D. drew in a ragged breath and damned himself for letting things get out of control with Kate. But his actions didn't surprise him—no, Kate could just about leave him senseless when she was around. He had to watch himself from now on. His life was manageable when things stood still, quiet, with no commotion. He'd had enough disruption to last a lifetime.

He needed to put Kate at a distance. She was too good for what he could offer. He rubbed his thumb and forefinger against his chin.

She's the kind of a woman who deserves a forever...a commitment...and for her and Charlie's sake, that was something he couldn't give her.

8

⟶ ⟵

"Kate, we've got problems."

The words dug into her dreamy consciousness and floated between the almost-tangible image of J.D. Through layers of muddled rhapsodies, strong fingers touched her arm, and she whispered encouragement. "Oh, yes that feels wonderful."

"Kate, the incubator's down."

The powerful, urgent tone forced her eyes to flutter open, and she gazed at J.D. not a foot away, his face serious and much too real. Struggling out of the abysmal sleep, she turned and blinked her eyes again. "Wha-what's the matter? What time is it?" she asked, her voice barely a whisper.

"Four. Alarm on the incubator went off about thirty minutes ago. We've got problems."

The message finally connected through her sleepiness, and she was aware of his hand on her shoulder. "The incubator. What's wrong with it?" She sat up and the thin cotton straps of her nightgown slipped down her bare arms, the lacy top inching over the curve of her breasts. A combination of uncertainty and energy flowed through her as she gazed at him.

"Incubator stopped working. Nothing's wrong with the electricity. Must be in the mechanism. The temperature is hot enough, but it won't stay that way. The eggs need to be turned every thirty minutes, or we're going to lose them.'' His voice was a whisper as he stood at the edge of her bed, his arms crossed over his chest and his brown hair tousled on his forehead.

Kate processed the information with closed eyes. J.D.'d warned her about problems with the incubator. The hatching device needed to be at least one hundred-and-four degrees and turning the eggs constantly. At last count there were over one hundred eggs in the incubator and more coming in daily. Losing that many hatchlings would set them back for months.

She shifted her gaze back to him and crossed her arms over her chest, now fully aware of J.D.'s gaze. ''What do we need to do?''

''I'm going out and take care of the pens. As soon as I'm finished, I'll collect the morning eggs. But the ones in the incubator need to be turned soon. I can't do it alone.'' He uncrossed his arms. ''Hated to wake you up so early, but...''

''Don't worry about it. We're partners, remember?'' She didn't hesitate to remind him of the fact. It had been a week since he'd tried to kiss her on the front porch, and they'd been avoiding each other. ''Just let me get dressed and pack a few things for Charlie, then I'll get down to the hatching barn.''

About to place her feet on the floor, she remembered the length of her gown and pulled the sheet up to her shoulders.

J.D.'s glance drifted over her, and even in the semidarkness she could see his eyes delighted in her. He walked over to the crib and placed his large hand on the railing. "Hate to wake the little guy."

"Don't worry about Charlie. He can go to sleep at the drop of a hat. I'll feed him down at the barn. Now just let me get dressed...." Even in the hurried, shadowy atmosphere he could make her cheeks burn.

"See you down at the barn."

Kate waited until he was out of sight, then stood and stretched, remembering her dream about him. The swirling memories assaulted and surrounded her senses like a mist slipping and inching its way into every pore. She shook her head. It would take half the morning to get over the sensual scenes her dreaming mind had conjured.

Kate pushed Charlie's stroller down the path to the hatching barn as the Texas sun tried to peek its head over the horizon. The cool, early morning mist hovered above the earth, drifting up to meet them.

She swung open the barn door and pushed her son into the familiar setting. The missing, steady hum of the incubator created a silent vacuum. Kate settled a sleeping Charlie at the far corner and headed for the quiet machine. Yawning, she tapped the thermometer. Ninety-seven degrees! The eggs wouldn't be safe if the temperature slipped any more. She turned to look at the humidity indicator. Thirteen percent. After weeks and months of monitoring the unit, Kate knew both readings were a big problem. Thank goodness, J.D. was home. At least he'd know what to do.

"Anything change?" J.D. asked as he entered the barn.

"No changes. The machine is dead as a doornail. What do we do?" Her gaze moved to him and her heart started pounding. Even with an emergency on their hands, Kate didn't fail to notice he'd already taken off his shirt. Seeing his taut bare skin, strong chest and muscled arms caused an intense flare of desire through her.

J.D. raked fingers across his thick, chestnut hair. "I've called the company, and they're sending someone out this afternoon, but that doesn't help us right now. We need to get the humidity back and keep the temperature up. We can't afford to lose all those eggs."

"That would be a total, financial disaster," Kate added.

"Exactly. We need heat and moisture."

Kate stepped to the incubator room and looked through the glass window. There had to be a way to heat the tiny area. She closed her eyes tightly and pressed her lips together. What in the world could they do? The idea popped into her mind almost automatically. "How about the heat lamps we used for the chicks the day Charlie was born? We could set them up and monitor the temperature. When it gets to one hundred and three, we can take a couple out and add a fan if we need to. Then do it all over again. I don't know what we're going to do about the humidity, though."

J.D.'s eyes brightened with a look she'd seen before. "Buckets of water with the heat lamps. The water will add the humidity we need." Standing beside her, he casually slipped an arm around her waist.

The natural warmth from his body burned through her thin top and twined its way to her heart, then plunged deeply and turned into special yearnings.

His arm tightened for a moment. "We'll work this

mess out. Just like we did the last time we were in a jam when Charlie was born," he said, tugging her even closer to him, giving her one last squeeze.

"Think so?" The question caught in her throat. Fighting more sexual undulation, she took a step back and broke his grasp. His words told her they were building a history together.

"Sure. You just watch. Ready to get to work?"

Kate's breath quickened. "Yes, but the eggs, they need to be turned."

"No problem, we'll work from the top down. Mark them with a pencil and turn them every half hour. We'll do it in shifts. Charlie eat yet?"

"No. He'll be ready in about half an hour."

J.D. smiled. "See, Charlie's cooperating. The plan is working already. You start turning. Mark the eggs with the time, then we'll know what's what. I'll set up the heat lamps and water. It's going to get mighty hot in there." Tapping the incubator's glass window with his fingernail, he turned back to her. His gaze traveled slowly and stopped at her breasts, which were straining the thin material.

She nodded her head and self-consciously swallowed. She'd thought enough to put on the skimpy tank top knowing she'd be working hard. But she hadn't thought about working so close to J.D. His gaze was glued to the curves the diminutive piece of clothing accented. Her body tingled with hostile energy—angry at herself for reacting so quickly to only a glance. "Let's get going," she stated, hoping the work alone would put an end to the silly feelings.

Kate turned the eggs carefully while J.D. set up the heat lamps. When the lamps were in place, her partner brought in water buckets and placed them in the four corners of the small enclosed room. Soon the area in and around the incubator was back up to the required temperature and humidity. They both grinned at each other with their success.

"See, the hardest part is over." J.D. wiped his forehead with his kerchief. "Hot as hell, but we've got it under control. How you doing?"

"I feel like I've been in a sauna, but half the eggs are turned." Kate drew her hand across her damp forehead. She stood and brushed against J.D.'s arm. The fine hair on his arm pressed her damp skin and sent a barrage of pinpoint-like sensations through her body.

Charlie's cry caused her to turn toward the stroller. "The bottomless pit needs his grub," she said.

Her partner laughed and stepped aside. "Don't worry about his eating habits. He's got to build up his weight for the Dallas Cowboys. When I'm old, I want free tickets. I know that kid's going to be a quarterback. Another Aikman."

"Wouldn't surprise me, the way he eats." She stepped away from the incubator and her muscles relaxed a little.

J.D. nodded toward the eggs. "I'll finish turning while you feed him."

The semicool air from the barn's open area refreshed her. Sitting in their usual place, she fed Charlie. Unaware of her present dilemma, her child cooed and gurgled happily between hungry gulps and burps. Comfortable, he didn't complain when she placed him back in the stroller. She called to J.D. to listen for him, and she ran up the path to the house.

She came back to the barn with her hands filled with plastic glasses of iced water. She was about to open the door to the barn when she heard J.D. talking to her son.

"Hey, little guy, you, me and your mama are working together just fine. When you get older, I'm gonna teach you all about the ranch. Maybe even buy you a pony to ride around." The words caused a deep ache in her heart. They were becoming like a family in many ways, yet she knew in reality it would never happen. They were on different paths. To stop the hurting in her chest she managed to pull the door open, and it squeaked.

"Here, you probably need this," she said as she handed him a large plastic cup.

"Thanks." J.D. stepped away from the stroller, gulped down the water quickly and some dripped down his chest. Glassy droplets traversed their way down, dissecting his tawny skin, tangling in the sprinkling of curly chestnut hair. An urgent need to trace their path and run her fingers through the tantalizing tufts blazed within her.

He cleared his throat, and her gaze snapped up to his. He stared at her. "Got the rest of the eggs turned. All we need to do right now is check on the humidity and heat. Really think this is going to work," he said.

They read the incubator dials together. The plan was working. They looked at each other and laughed.

J.D.'s cheeks were flushed and his skin covered with a glistening sheen, looking much like she'd remembered from her dream earlier—like he'd just made feverous love to her. She shook her damp hair and took a step back, remembering her promise to herself and her son.

Hours later, after the repair man had fixed the incubator and gone, they jumped up and down like little kids, hugging and kissing each other. They giggled and admired Charlie. J.D. picked up Charlie and explained to him Kate's talent.

They cavorted up the dusty, moonlit path, J.D. carrying Charlie. Halfway to the house, Kate realized his arm was around her, and to outside eyes they looked very much like a family.

J.D. searched through the kitchen cabinets, looking for one last item. Yesterday had turned into thirteen hours of hard work before the incubator was fixed. He, Kate and Charlie had gotten back to the house at eighty-thirty, all three exhausted but satisfied. Pride welled up in his heart. Kate had been a trooper. He couldn't have saved the eggs by himself.

Hell, she was the one who had thought of how to save them! This morning when he woke up, he'd felt the same sensations he'd experienced yesterday and last night. A sexual craving he found impossible to deny.

Shuffling through another cabinet, he spied what he was looking for: holders for the candles he'd already laid on the table. He'd decided midmorning to cook Kate a special dinner to celebrate their victory. It was the least he could do. He'd given her so much grief when she'd first come to the ranch, and now, he realized he was better off that she'd stayed.

She deserved a thank-you.

Yeah, right, Pruitt! Tell yourself something you'll believe.

The thought ripped through his rationale. He *did* want to do something special for her. But wanting to be with her was the driving factor. An hour ago he'd sent her from the kitchen demanding she take a nice, long bath and relax while he fed Charlie. And when she'd appeared before he was ready, he'd suggested she go put on something pretty for her *surprise*. A happy look had appeared in her eyes at the word and made him feel a bit guilty. Yeah, it was a surprise for her, but he wasn't sure all the planning was just for Kate.

He'd been trying so hard to stay away from her after the episode on the porch, that he'd swung himself to the other side of the continuum with the illogical logic that he could get her out of his mind if he ignored her. Yesterday had proved to him *that* was impossible.

He placed the candlesticks on the table, reorganized the wineglasses and lined up the knives, forks and spoons. He wasn't fixing anything fancy— steaks, baked potatoes, both cooked on the grill, and cherry pie he'd purchased at the grocery.

"Hey, can I give you a hand?" she asked, entering the kitchen.

"Nope, everything's under control. Fixing you the best steak and baked potato within fifty miles." He juggled two large potatoes and caught them in midair. "And if you've got a good appetite, dessert."

A frown grew on her face. "This really isn't necessary," she said. She sat at the kitchen table and crossed her legs. Although she protested his dinner offer, she'd accepted his suggestion and put on a pretty yellow sundress he'd never seen before. Her familiar sweet perfume wafted up and curled under his nose.

"Know it isn't, but you'll just have to enjoy it. Indulge me, will you?" he stated, smiling and winking. "Is Charlie asleep?"

Kate looked up at him quizzically. "He fell asleep a few minutes ago. Probably'll sleep like a rock. I don't think I've seen him so tired."

She'd applied a small amount of makeup to enhance her green eyes and her lips, and the effect was irresistible. He took the chilled bottle of wine out of the refrigerator, uncorked it and poured her a small amount.

Lifting her glass, she swirled the wine then tasted it. "Very good," Kate said, and held out her glass.

J.D. filled it and his own almost to the rim. "To a successful rescue," he announced, and clicked his glass with hers.

Kate sipped her wine while J.D. cooked the steaks to perfection. Then they ate slowly, enjoying the food and conversation. When they finished dinner, both cleared the table and stacked the few dishes, and soon they were sitting on the couch in the living room.

"If I'd known you could cook so well, I'd have let you help me in the kitchen more," Kate said, pulling her bare feet underneath her. She leaned back and sighed.

J.D. noted that in the soft light she looked more than beautiful. "Sorry, but you've seen it all. Steak and baked potatoes, my only claim to fame. Get mighty tired of them if that's all we had." Sitting so close to her on the couch stretched his imagination. He was acutely aware of her quiet, gentle breathing, and the easy rise and fall of her chest. His imagination worked overtime and soon his fingers were stroking her breasts, letting his hands slide over her stomach and—

"J.D.?"

The sound of his name broke into his thoughts, and he dragged himself away from the pleasurable image.

Good Lord, how he wanted the woman sitting next to him.

"Yeah?" He wasn't surprised at his daydream. They'd been through a lot since she'd arrived on his doorstep a few months ago, and the journey had knocked down certain emotional walls he'd built. Walls he didn't think could be demolished by a bulldozer.

"Thank you for dinner. It was very good," she murmured.

Her sweet voice sent his blood pulsing to his extremities. Even in his first youthful infatuation with Ann, he'd never felt so fully enamored. J.D. drew in a breath and tried to keep from sliding an arm around her, but he didn't succeed. His limb went around her shoulders. The action caused an upheaval in him that was comparable to a volcano. To his surprise, she didn't pull from his caress, and the mist of desire that floated up from the fire beneath his belly blinded him of anything but one fact.

He was at the point of no return.

Kate felt his arm against her shoulders, but she didn't respond as she expected herself to do—she nestled into his embrace. Yet the rational part of her mind fought her all the way.

You're asking for trouble, just wait.

Before she could force herself to move away, he cupped her bare arm with his warm hand, his fingers kneaded the small muscles. Kate didn't have to tell herself again she should get as far away from him as possible.

No, she knew!

But her clearheaded thoughts had been stripped away by the small amount of wine and J.D.'s attention. She placed her hand against the material of the couch, and his fingers surrounded her shoulder again. As she tried to pull away, she made the mistake of turning and meeting his gaze. When she saw the craving in his eyes, she was lost. How could she fight what she didn't want to fight? How could she stop her own desires when they encircled gracefully and melted her arguments? With a sigh she took a deep breath and stopped fighting.

J.D. ran his hand down her shoulder then brought it back to lace his fingers through her hair. Lowering his head to hers, he kissed her mouth lightly yet seductively. His lips slid to her temple, and he kissed a path to each eyelid and trailed a set of kisses along her jaw.

Kate thread her fingers through his hair and pulled him toward her open mouth, wanting more of him. Their lips met and tongues danced while he pressed her closer. He brought his mouth away from hers for one brief moment. "I've been waiting for this for a long time." His voice, already husky, grew thicker. "It's going to be good with us."

His mouth covered hers again, unrelenting and marauding, seizing full possession of her lips. Again he crushed her tightly against him, one hand holding her head, the other slipping her back onto the couch.

Wildly, Kate felt her entire being catch fire. A storm of emotion swept through her, and she held him closer as his hard body pressed to hers.

Slipping the thin straps of her sundress from her shoulders, he ran hungry hands over her back, then around front to cup her covered breasts. When his thumbs found her sensitive nipples through the thin material, a growl slipped from the back of his throat.

Kate shivered. Part of her wanted to stop him, and yet the other half never wanted anything more, and the confusion caused a mixture of pleasure and pain. Tenderness pulsed in her heart for him. She wanted to—no, *needed* to be a part of him. She'd never experienced such needs before. They came together like fire and air and fed on each other, creating a flaming storm of desire. She laced her arms around him and gently kissed the arch of his neck.

"Kate, we've waited a long time." His voice reminded her of the dark red wine they'd just enjoyed.

The sexually induced euphoria enveloped them, and he traced his tongue down her throat. His mouth found hers again, his tongue searching. They mingled together like warm honey and butter.

"You're so beautiful," he whispered as he stared down at her. His hands cupped her breasts again, and she leaned into him. "I want you, like I've never wanted anyone, Kate," he whispered, stroking the orbs tenderly. "You know that, don't you?"

Yes, she knew. She could see it in his gaze and feel it in his touch, yet she still hesitated and wondered. There were reasons—hard-found and soul-burning reasons not to continue. But she didn't want to stop. In fact, she wanted to encourage him, make him feel as she did right now…and…love him.

His hands tantalized her, and a knife-throbbing ache reached her belly as a seductive fire raged between her legs, spinning her thoughts out of control. Fingers found the flat of her stomach and moved farther down, swirling and teasing. The intensity caused her to tremble. She ignored the hurt and pain that had been stored and stacked like ammunition to keep anyone away who got too close to her heart.

The rawness of their yearnings melted and fused them together into one, and Kate clung to him as they kissed passionately. Each kiss growing deeper and hotter, more intimate than the one before. Blistering swells of arousal washed over them.

And just as they'd found a rhythm in everything they did together—working, playing and bringing Charlie into the world, they created an intimate secret language all their own.

He tangled his fingers in her hair and tugged at it. She opened her eyes and looked into his. "I knew it'd be like this for us," he growled, the sensual ruddiness of his voice stroked against her rawness like a caress.

Minutes later she pulled her mouth away from his. "I love you, J.D.," she whispered as the magic of their blending whirled her to a sensual realm of intensity. The words brought a sharp apprehension and it tore through her, replacing the sensual passion.

She couldn't retrieve the three small words. How could she love J.D. after all she'd promised herself and her child? They were partners in the Circle C—not lovers.

His rapturous kisses stole the searing thought away and tossed it above them. She let herself respond to him again, kissing him with all her might. Suddenly rational thought came back to her. She owed it to her son and herself to use all her self-control. She needed to be strong and fight her desire for J.D. She didn't need to love him. What she had to find was independence and a life of her own. Once they became lovers, their relationship would change. Their business partnership would dissolve into a mass of intricate, confusing emotions filled with problems.

Lovers never last.

And then what would she have? Broken memories and a shattered heart. She'd never put her heart on the line again—she had to stay safe for Charlie, but most of all for herself.

She felt herself push away from him, her hands on his chest. "I can't, J.D." Was all she could say before her voice cracked.

His flushed face, filled with surprise, met her gaze as he tried to pull her back into his arms. Foreboding tore through her thoughts and body and gave her a strength she didn't know she possessed. "I'm sorry...J.D." She stood, pulling the straps of her sundress onto her shoulders, her breasts tingling. Knowing she'd be helpless if she looked at him again, she quickly turned and ran to her room.

9

—◆—

"Herman, I swear I could kick you," Kate yelled across the pen. She'd just come from the hatching barn where she'd candled three of Jezabel's eggs. There wasn't a fertile one among them. Glancing to the far end of the pen, she saw the two birds standing next to each other. "You two better decide you like each other soon, or there's going to be trouble around here, and neither one of you is going to like it!"

Shaking the mop head at both of them, she marched across the pen, opened the gate, stepped out and slammed it shut. The noise startled Charlie, who was in his stroller, and he looked up at his mother, eyes filled with surprise.

"Sorry, baby. Mama's just mad at those two stubborn birds. They need to do what comes naturally, or we're going to see them both on the dinner table in a few days." Kate knelt down by the stroller and patted her son's tummy. His green eyes relaxed and a tiny toothless smile forced the corners of his mouth to turn up.

"Charlie, you're a flirt," Kate chimed, and tickled him under the chin. He responded with another grin, then stuck his tongue out and made sucking noises. Laughing, she searched for the thing her son loved best. After popping a pacifier in his mouth, she watched it bob up and down. He'd be hungry for his breakfast in a few minutes. Just one more pen to collect eggs from, and she could feed him.

Kate looked up toward the driveway at the right side of the house. J.D. had taken off early this morning for ostrich feed and was due back soon. He'd argued with her last night about going so early, knowing that Charlie would have to be taken down to the pens when she collected the eggs. But she insisted, saying they'd be fine, and he needed to get the heavy, time-consuming work done before the sun and humidity got too high. J.D. had conceded and left before dawn.

She pressed her lips together, wishing the man wouldn't act so protective toward them. It only made him that much more attractive. And with all her heart she needed to deny any attraction at all. But denying what she felt for J.D. was getting more difficult with each moment.

Even though they acted as if nothing had happened the other night when they'd found themselves on the couch, the atmosphere between them was still strong and sensual. Sure they spoke when they needed to and were polite, but they danced around each other like two unsure cats. And neither said a word about the passionate fire that kept building between them.

An uncomfortable laugh fell from her lips, and she cursed the rush of blood to her cheeks. After the other night, what must he think of her? The startled look on his face when she'd pulled away, made her shudder. He probably thought... She didn't even want to think about what he thought. She'd let him kiss her and had kissed him back.

Oh, God, did I kiss him.

Her fingertips went to her lips and traced across

them. His kisses had done something, had fanned the raging yearning in her she didn't dare deny. And the three little words that had come careening out of her mouth as if they'd had a mind of their own... *I love you.*

Her face flushed again. Did she love J.D.? She wasn't sure she could answer that question, or wanted to. Thank goodness, reason had taken control. It would have been so easy to convince herself to continue.

She shook her head and laughed again, mad at herself for being so silly. It had been nothing more than a kiss going out of control, that was all. She stopped laughing and drew in another quick breath and corrected herself.

No, it hadn't been just a kiss and losing control, she reminded herself. No, it had been more emotion than she ever felt before, and it was too late to even try to fool herself.

My goodness, she'd actually told the man she loved him.

The memory of her words floated back and stoked the growing fire within her. Why in the world had she said those words?

She didn't love J. D. Pruitt—that was ridiculous. There were times she didn't even like him. The thought caught in the back of her mind and she smiled.

That wasn't true, either.

She liked him a lot, even if he did make her mad sometimes, but love... She sighed. She was so mixed up.

If she just hadn't kissed him!

Kate pushed the stroller down to the next pen. Controlling her silly feelings and getting her mind on the business of running the ranch and raising her son was the answer to the way she felt right now. She worked to steady her breathing and vowed to think of other things. There was a lot of work to finish today, and daydreaming about J.D. wasn't going to get the work done.

In front of the last pen she brought the stroller to a stop and locked the wheels. "Mama'll be right back, and then I'll get my big boy some breakfast," she cooed at Charlie, and made sure the top on the stroller was positioned to shield him from the rising sun. He answered her by clamping onto his pacifier and sucking with all his might.

"Oh, darn," Kate said to herself as she looked around for the mop head. Looking up the path, she shook her head. She'd been so busy thinking about J.D., she'd left it at Herman's pen. If she went into the last pen quickly, instead of going back and getting her protection, she'd be finished sooner, and then she could feed Charlie. Glancing into the pen she saw that both ostriches were at the far corner, engrossed in the last of their feed. She looked back at her son. Charlie gurgled and grinned up at her. He was such a patient child, she hated to make him wait any longer.

Opening the gate quietly, Kate slipped through. She'd get the egg and be out in a matter of seconds. Reaching the nest, she found not one but two eggs. Picking one up, she cradled it in her left arm. Before she could reach for the second egg, she heard the distinct scuttling of a bird. Standing up straight, she whirled around and came face to breast with the rooster who'd obviously spotted her. He stalked across the small area in front of the nest.

Her heart pounded against her chest as she tried

to think of what J.D. had said. He'd warned her about getting cornered by a male and demanded she never go into a pen without her mop contraption. Fear knotted in her stomach and took all her rational thoughts away. The bird eyed her curiously and then strutted · his dusty territory, kicking up gravel.

"Shoo, shoo," she yelled, swinging her free arm. The words and action only seemed to agitate the bird, and he looked down, lids blinking slowly over his large eyes.

Instantly, she decided to make a run for it. She dropped the egg to the ground, and it rolled past her feet. She kicked it toward the bird. The harsh movement didn't even crack the strong shell, and the angry rooster ignored it.

Edging toward the fence, her heart pounded and panic caused her breath to come faster. She broke into a run toward the gate and could feel the bird close at her heels. With her hand on the latch, she pulled it up. A bone-crushing thud to the right side of her body forced a scream from her. She felt a dull yet piercing ache in her arm, and the last thing she heard was Charlie's hungry cry.

J.D. whistled along with Garth Brooks and the best country-western song he'd heard in a long time. He and the truckful of feed bounced on the notoriously bumpy road the Texas Highway Department offered as their best. He'd gotten the feed loaded sooner than he'd expected, and now he was driving down Main Street. His plan was to stop for a cup of coffee at the Sunshine Café and then head out to the ranch.

He checked his watch. Kate should be just finishing collecting the eggs from the pens. Probably feeding Charlie and having another cup of coffee. The vision of Charlie and Kate came into his mind, and he smiled and turned up the radio. God, how they had changed his way of living.

He chuckled as he thought of all the cute things Charlie did. The kid, just looking at him, could make him feel like a million dollars. He was a great little guy.

And his mother...an image of Kate came into his mind. His stomach tightened, and his mouth went dry. He reached to the dashboard and turned up the radio. She had him so mixed up with emotion he didn't know if he was sure how he felt. Garth Brooks drawled the words to his song, and J.D. set his jaw. Why kid himself? He knew how he felt about Kate.

The acknowledgment of his feelings caused beads of perspiration to form on his forehead. The other night he'd let his physical needs run away from him. But how could he stop himself? Kate had looked so beautiful sitting beside him, he'd forgotten what he'd promised himself long ago when Ann died.

Thank God, Kate had come to her senses when she did and pulled out of his arms. He wouldn't have stopped kissing her for anything.

He pulled the truck into a parking space outside the Sunshine, but didn't turn off the engine. Garth sang and J.D.'s memory whipped up the same feelings he'd experienced with Kate in his arms.

He twisted the key in the ignition and the country love song cut in two. J.D. pulled the key out and opened the truck door. He had to remember Kate wanted only to be partners—nothing more. He sucked in a breath and reminded himself of something else. They had to get away from him—for their sake alone.

* * *

Charlie's cry tore through her murky consciousness, and she tried to lift her head and shake the clouded swelling that kept her from moving back into reality. With all the strength she could muster, she forced her eyelids open. Kate blinked, her eyelashes fluttering against the dust and gravel. She remembered the last thing she'd felt—a slamming against her arm and side that had knocked her to the ground with a power much like a Mack truck colliding into a fragile cinder wall.

Her child's cry grew louder. A blurry outline of two ostriches came into semifocus. Both stood at the opposite end of the pen. A penetrating, sharp pain ran the length of her arm as she tried to push herself up but fell back to the ground.

"Damn it, Kate, what the hell happened? Where are you hurt?"

The familiar voice forced her eyes opened again. A double image of J.D. danced before her. She felt his face close to hers, his hand on her shoulder.

Wetting her parched lips, her voice echoed in her own ears and she moaned. "Charlie...where's Charlie?"

"He's okay. Hungry, but I'll get some food in him soon. Don't worry...don't worry about anything."

In a haze she felt him pick her up and cradle her in his arms. Depleted of any energy, she let her cheek fall against his chest. How long had she been lying on the ground? How long had Charlie been crying for her? She twisted in J.D.'s arms, and shafts of agony hammered against fragile nerves.

As worry about Charlie crawled in her mind, she vaguely knew J.D. was carrying her up the path.

* * *

J.D. sat in the cramped hospital waiting room, his elbows resting on his thighs, hands gripped together and head held against his palms. After finding Kate lying unconscious facedown in the dirt, he didn't think anything worse could happen.

He'd heard Charlie howling when he pulled the truck in the driveway and smiled to himself. The little guy ate like a linebacker—he was probably hungry. Then when the crying had gone on for more than a few minutes, he ran down the path to where he thought the noise was coming from, worry churning his gut.

That's when he'd seen the stroller on the dusty path shaking with Charlie's sobs. Kate would never leave him alone or let him work himself into such a crying fit. It had taken him ten full seconds to find her, and those moments had been the longest ten seconds of his life.

The minute he saw her crumpled against the fence, he knew what had happened. A reckless anger stole any calmness he possessed, yet he picked her up as gently as possible.

When she was secure in his arms, he raced out of the pen to the stroller. He managed to push Charlie up the path while he cradled Kate in his arms. The bumping and speed had stopped Charlie from crying for a few moments, and the baby looked up at J.D. with helpless green eyes as they barreled to the truck.

He drove into town, his foot pressing the gas pedal to the floor, tires squealing, feed spilling out the back. Kate leaned against his shoulder and he steadied Charlie against his right thigh while the baby screamed his lungs out. With each jar in the road, she moaned, pain etched and buried on her delicate face. Three blocks before he reached the hospital, he started honking the truck's horn, and by the time he reached the emergency entrance, a nurse was standing out in front trying to figure out what was going on.

High heels tapping against the hospital linoleum brought him out of the haze of dread he felt.

"James Dean," Meg said gently as she stood in front of him in the hallway. Although he heard his name, he didn't pull his gaze up. Still trying to focus his eyes, he worked to control the sinking feeling in his gut.

Charlie's blanket lay in a lump on the floor between his legs, the bright yellow chicken design flashing at him. After the nurses had gotten Kate on a gurney and rolled her into the emergency room, another nurse had taken the screaming Charlie out of his arms and had said something about feeding him and changing his diaper.

J.D. swallowed hard. He had no idea how Charlie was, or what was going to happen to Kate. The acid, antiseptic hospital smells assaulted him, reminding him of the only other time he'd been in the same emergency room, waiting for someone to tell him what had happened to his wife.

"James Dean, are you all right?" Meg asked, still standing in front of him, her hand now on his shoulder.

He couldn't speak. The dryness in his throat kept him from doing so. He fully expected Meg's eyes to be red and rimmed with tears. Knowing he couldn't prolong the inevitable, he drew his gaze to his cousin's.

"She's going to be okay," Meg stated, her hand still on his shoulder.

"What?"

"She's got a broken arm, two right ribs are cracked, and her right side is bruised badly, but all things considered, it could have been a lot worse. My God, that freaking bird could have killed her. She's a lucky woman."

The news rushed through him like a tornado. The last twenty-five minutes sitting in the metal hospital chair had been spent worrying about something far worse. Kate was going to be all right. She wasn't paralyzed or dead. But too soon, guilt saturated the places that were left, and a sick wave of confusion rolled over him.

"What's going to happen now?" he asked. Chilled, reprehensible thoughts echoed through his mind—recriminations forcing his mouth back into a grim line.

"We've got to set her arm and put a cast on. Then tape her ribs. She'll have to stay in the hospital for a few days. After, she can go home and rest. I've sedated her, and as soon as we've got the operating room ready—"

"If she's okay, why a few days?" He stood, wondering if his legs would hold him.

"I want her under observation just to make sure there's no internal injuries. That animal kicked her a good one. She needs to be on a painkiller for a while, too. Her arm's a clean break, but that together with the ribs...she'll be in a lot of pain. Everything should be healed in about four weeks."

"It's my fault," he said abruptly, angry at himself that it had taken him so long to admit the truth. He crumbled into the chair, in the same position he'd been in a few minutes before, but this time his face muscles were so tight it made his jaw hurt.

Meg sat next to him, her hand back on his shoulder. "I don't think it's anybody's fault. Accidents happen."

"Yeah. Right! While I was sitting having a cup of coffee in town, Kate was lying in the dust, practically dead, and Charlie was squalling his lungs out." He let out a puff of air, disgusted with himself.

"You didn't know what was going on—"

"Not an excuse." His hand sliced the air. "Shouldn't have left so early, but figured it would be easier. That's what I get for thinking." His voice dropped to a snarl.

Meg stood, her hands on her hips, a determined look on her face. "Well, you can sit here and blame yourself or you can come in and give her some encouragement if you want."

He stood again, his legs more shaky than they'd been before. "Yeah, you're right. I need to see her." He quickly glanced around the room. "Where's Charlie? Is he okay?"

Meg's arm laced through his and she grabbed his hand. "He's fine. Gladys took him down to Pediatrics. I wanted him checked out. After he had his bottle and got a dry diaper, he went right to sleep. Of course not until every nurse on the floor held him, and Gladys personally rocked him. You can see him after we check on Kate."

They walked toward the double swinging doors, Meg leading the way. J.D. fought the sick feeling in his stomach as more anger grew in his chest. Kate was lying in the hospital because of him and nobody was going to convince him of anything different.

His cousin pulled back the white curtain, and J.D. stared at Kate. Her auburn hair was a tangled mass of curls on the stark white pillow. Small scratches on one side of her face formed a red, swollen crisscross pattern.

For a moment there was only silence, and then Kate groaned, twisted from side to side and muttered something about Charlie. Shock at seeing her so helpless again quickly worked its way into a fury, and he swallowed back the bile. He pulled his fingers into tight fists, afraid if he let himself feel anything at all, he'd damage something.

"Hey, kiddo. You've got a visitor," Meg said softly, letting her fingers feather across her patient's forehead.

Kate stirred, her eyes fluttering open, a dazed faraway look appearing in them. Her tongue darted out and wet her dry lips. "Hi," she whispered.

J.D. stepped forward, unfurled his hand and automatically brought it to her cheek. Unable to take his hand away, he let it rest there.

"Kate, you'll be just fine," he said, wondering where the words were coming from. He wanted to bring her into his arms, and hold her, make it early this morning when there might be time to protect her.

She nodded ever so slightly, and tried to smile, but a grimace slid into its place. "Charlie, is he…" She bit her bottom lip, not able to continue, her eyes shiny with tears.

J.D. combed through her hairline, hoping to soothe her in some way. "Hey, you don't worry about that little guy, I'll take care of him. He's down in the nursery right now getting the royal treatment and all the attention he could want. He just needs his mama to get better. That's all you need to worry about." His voice had dropped to barely a rasp.

Damn it, he couldn't stand to see her this way.

She acknowledged his encouragement with a nod and then closed her eyes again.

"Better let her get some rest. We need to set her arm soon. Why don't you go home and get some rest yourself?" Meg suggested as she led the way out.

"I'm not leaving until I know she's okay," J.D. stated stubbornly, and flopped back in the chair Meg had found him in.

"That's probably a better idea. Her arm won't take long, then all she needs is some sleep. If everything is okay, she can go home day after tomorrow."

J.D. nodded, not able to think beyond Kate getting through surgery. "And Charlie...."

"He's a little toughie. He can stay in the nursery until Kate leaves. Might be easier for you. The ranch needs you, too."

J.D. rubbed the heel of his hand against his chin. "Nah, if it's okay, I'll take him home with me after Kate's in recovery."

"No problem. That would be better for him. He needs to be in a familiar environment. Think you can handle it?"

He nodded again. "I'll go to the Baker ranch and borrow one of their workers. Heard their son John is home from college. Probably have a spare hand around."

Meg smiled. "Everything is going to work out, James Dean." She turned and walked back to the emergency room.

10

Kate came through the setting of her broken arm without a hitch. After staying with her for an hour, J.D. drove out to the Baker Ranch and made arrangements for an extra hand to come over to the Circle C for the rest of the month. Stopping back by the ranch, he completed the major chores, found Charlie's car seat and then drove back to the hospital. He dropped by the nursery to tell Gladys he'd be taking the baby home in a while. He did it all as if walking through a nightmare, not feeling, hearing or smelling anything.

Then he went to see her again. She lay sleeping among the crisp white sheets, motionless, her breath moving in and out of her chest in obvious painful measures. The deep, blood-red scratches from scraping her face against the ground blazed on her pale skin. He stood over the bed, staring down at her for what seemed to be an eternity.

The first time he'd seen her face, he'd thought she was spunky and the prettiest woman he'd ever set eyes on. Now, as he gazed down at her, he realized how much he'd learned about her in the last few months.

The spunkiness was really courage he admired, and the attitude happened to be a protective mechanism she'd built after the disappointment her ex-husband caused. He took her unharmed hand between his thumb and fingers and massaged it tenderly. She stirred and mumbled and then settled into a dreamless rest.

She'd been determined to work the ranch and had done a good job. She helped him beyond what he ever thought possible. Her positive perspective and her well-thought-out ideas had saved them thousands of dollars and time.

And she brought happiness into his life.

Kate Owens.

He let the name roll around in his numb mind for a few moments. His gaze stayed fixed on her face. Seeing that she was resting peacefully made him smile. She was going to be okay and the knowledge shaved a tiny piece of the worry from the huge mound that gnawed in his stomach.

She could have been killed, and Charlie, too. The memory of Charlie's unanswered cries echoed in his thoughts and caused more torment to surge through his body.

Fisting his free hand, he knew he had to stop thinking this way—letting an immeasurable hurt grow within him. If he let the hurt go on, it would surely turn into an anger that was difficult to control. An anger that made him see that his fate was responsible for what happened to her.

"She won't be waking up for a while," the nurse on duty said as she passed by the open door. "The sedative the doctor gave her is pretty potent. Why don't you go home and get some rest?"

J.D.'s gaze shifted to the door. The nurse smiled sweetly and continued on her mission. He needed to get Charlie back to the ranch and comfortable in his own bed, but he didn't want to leave Kate.

He looked at her one more time—not needing to memorize her face. He'd already done that months back. How could he forget her eyes or her smile? The way she pressed her lips together when she was thinking about something important, or her laugh when she found his bad jokes funny. Or how her little finger always crooked around her coffee mug in the morning. How the small sexy sound came from her throat when they'd kissed.

He shook his head, knowing what he had to do. He placed her hand back on the bed and headed for the door.

When he got home he settled Charlie in his crib then stood at the side, leaning on the railing, just staring at him. His tiny face held a world of innocence. He'd grown to love the little guy—as if he was his own. The house was museum quiet and he could hear Charlie's tiny respirations against the emptiness. He'd wanted to protect them both, but he'd failed.

Sure that Charlie was sound asleep, he walked to his room and found the dusty cardboard box that had been shoved back on a deep shelf five years ago. With Kate laying in the hospital with broken bones and Charlie without his mother, J.D. needed to remind himself of what his life was all about.

He sat on the bed and pulled the lid off the yellowing box. Petals from a now brown, dried flower Ann had saved sifted through his fingers and fell to the floor. Remainders of a flower he'd given her on prom night she couldn't bring herself to throw away. His gold wedding band rolled in the box. Ann had picked it out in Fort Worth. Their ten-year-old marriage license with Ann's shaky signature, barely readable, glared back at him.

Pictures of Ann and himself fell on the bed, and he examined each one, brushing the tips of his fingers across the distorted likenesses. Images of them so happy they looked as if they were both about to burst with love.

They'd experienced a simple love, young and pure. Hell, he wasn't even sure they would have lasted ten years, they were so young. He loved Ann—there was no denying that fact—but he also knew his feelings for Kate had gone far beyond what, as a young kid, he'd felt for Ann.

And that's what bothered him most of all.

He needed to remind himself what he'd known for a long time. He was the reason Ann was gone. Plain and simple.

He picked up the only picture he had of his father. The obscure image stared back at him. His luck had gone bad a long time back when his father had taken off on him and his mother. Anyone who dared to love him experienced the bad luck, too. Today had proved and reinforced what he believed and knew. He was a bad-luck charm for any woman who had the hapless misfortune to love James Dean Pruitt.

Kate'd claimed her love the night on the couch in their moment of passion, and he could see it in her eyes, in her voice and the way she kissed him. A woman like Kate didn't give herself away with such abandon without loving deeply.

He stood and shoved his memories back into the musty box and placed it where it belonged—in a dark hiding place. He wouldn't put Kate or Charlie in jeopardy. When he shut the door on the reminders he'd so carefully let himself forget, a very clear realization sheared through him. He loved Kate and Charlie too much to let this continue. He had to get her off the ranch for her own sake and for Charlie's, too. Make sure she hated him enough so she'd never come back.

Their partnership had to end.

"Your arm okay?" J.D. asked after he chewed and swallowed the last bite of meat loaf. It was the first question he'd bothered to ask her in a month. They'd spent a silent twenty minutes eating dinner, and Kate was now used to J.D.'s sullen ways. Tonight she'd ventured to ask a few questions at first, and J.D. had grunted a cursory answer and went back to staring at his dinner plate.

"When Meg cut the cast off this morning she said it's as good as new." She flexed her hand back and forth to prove her point. "I can start collecting eggs tomorrow, and maybe I can pick up a few more chores, too. You've been pulling more than your share. I feel terrible about having to hire extra help."

"Won't be necessary. We've got it under control." J.D. banged his knife and fork on the plate, crumpled his paper napkin and threw it on the table.

"But I enjoy collecting the eggs. If you're worried about another accident, I assure you it's not a problem. I've learned my lesson." She stopped when she noticed J.D. wasn't even listening to her, or if he was, he didn't believe what she was saying.

She stood and picked up both plates and walked to the sink. Unable to contain her anger and humiliation, she turned back to speak to him. His chair was empty. The back door slammed. Any embarrassment she was feeling quickly gave way to hot anger. Slamming the dishes in the sink, she twisted the handle for hot water. She didn't understand what was going on between them, but tonight she was determined to find out.

Her heart raced with anticipation. After she washed the dishes and put Charlie to bed, she walked out to the front porch. That's where he'd been spending most of his evenings for the past weeks since she'd come home from the hospital.

He was sitting in the very spot where they'd kissed months ago. Her heart pounded as she closed the screen door and walked to stand across from him. His hair was mussed, dark circles rimmed his eyes and deep lines etched his face. An empty crumpled beer can sat beside him and he held another up to his mouth. He looked up at her, his eyes blank.

"I need to talk to you." Her voice was stern.

"I'm busy right now," he said, the tone of his voice flat.

"No, you aren't." She glared at him, still wondering what the heck was going on.

He shook his head, shifted his gaze away from her to his hand and then he stared out into the dark open space of the front yard. His steady, labored breathing filled the air.

She bit her bottom lip. He always expanded his chest when he had a problem.

He turned back to face her, his mouth forming into a tight line, a look of frustration growing in his eyes. "Okay, you want to talk. Feel free." He stood and stepped to the far end of the porch, positioning himself on the banister.

She drew in a determined breath, then blew it out. "I want to know what's the matter with you." There, she'd said it, and like the cast coming off her arm, it was a great release.

"Not a thing, except I want you off the ranch."

"What?" Kate stared at J.D., deciding she'd either mistaken what he'd said or she was dreaming.

He took another long gulp of his beer and then looked at her in the bright porch light. His eyes narrowed and frustration grew on his face. "You and Charlie need to move."

She heard the words this time correctly, but it took her long seconds to put them together. He hadn't said why or even asked her if she wanted to move. No, he was sitting on the opposite side of the porch with a smirk on his lips demanding that she leave the Circle C.

"I think you've had too many beers." She clenched and unclenched her fists, then knotted them again and dug her fingernails into her fleshy palms. Anger hammered against her skull, yet to her surprise she remained calm.

"Not enough, actually." He finished off his beer and crushed the can in one hand.

"Then you must have forgotten what we talked about months ago."

He snickered, and she wanted to slap the smile off his face. "Haven't forgotten a thing."

Kate's thoughts traced back over the past few months and she grew more confused. Sure, they'd started out rocky, but they'd worked into sharing the ranch and had fun in the process. "I feel like I'm having a bad dream."

"You're not. Been thinking for a while about you and Charlie leaving. Good idea," he rumbled. "Why's that so hard for you to understand?" He glared at her.

His condescending attitude was too much. "You tell me!"

"Not in the mood for word games," he said.

"I'm not playing word games. The reason I can't understand this whole mess...." she stuttered and stopped. "What about what we've gone through? I thought we were partners...it all ends so quickly for you just because I got hurt?"

He shrugged his shoulders and dropped his gaze. "Everything has to end sometime or another." The words came out in a mumble, but she understood every word.

"Is that the way you really feel?" Her eyes grew wider, and she couldn't help but stare at him.

A rooster boomed twice and then stillness surrounded them. He caught her gaze. Without blinking, his eyes glazed over, and his mouth dropped half open. "Yeah, that's the way I really feel. Time you left the Circle C. I need the room, and you're not that much help. Plus the kid cries all the time. When I decided to let you stay here, you knew it wouldn't be forever. If you hadn't broken your arm, I would have asked you to leave even sooner."

She stood in the middle of the porch staring at him. Too dazed to control her anger, she bit her lip to hold back a scream. She wouldn't allow him to see her out of control. No, she wouldn't give him that.

"I'm afraid you're forgetting one thing. Just like before. I own half this ranch, and I don't plan to leave it. Like I told you when we first met, you can leave just as easily as I can. Now it's even easier because I know how to run the entire ranch. Probably better than you."

She placed her hands on her hips and pressed

down as hard as she could to keep her outrage within, afraid of what she might do if she let go. "I'm not giving up the ranch and you'd just better get used to the idea." Not wanting to give him any more, she turned on one heel and made her way back into the house.

At the kitchen sink she poured a glass of water and drank it down slowly, wishing the trembling would go away. How could she have been so terribly stupid and naive? Of course he wanted her off the ranch. The sick numbness made her dizzy. It wasn't that she didn't believe what had just happened. No, she believed it with all her heart, but she was mad at herself for being so obtuse—he hadn't changed at all.

She placed the empty glass on the counter. Well, if she was going to start over again, there was no time like the present. Maybe he wanted her off the ranch, but that was just tough.

He cleared his throat, and she turned around to face him in the bright kitchen light. Holding a thick folder in his hand, he stepped to the kitchen table and set it down. "Think you better have a look at the agreement your uncle and I signed before you go telling me you're not leaving." His words were flat and dry and full of common sense.

"I don't need to look at any of that. I've already made up my mind, I'm staying, and if you don't like it, too bad," she said, the stubbornness growing in her tone. "I'm not leaving."

He ignored her and opened the file and flipped through the paperwork. Finding what he was looking for, he picked it out of the pile and handed it to her.

She snatched the paper out of his hand and read the title. It was the ownership agreement between

J.D. and her uncle. "What's this supposed to do? I know you and my uncle owned the ranch together." She tried to hand it back to him, but he shoved his hands into his jeans. "Well?"

"Read the fifth paragraph." His eyes were as dull as they were out on the porch.

She scanned the paragraph but couldn't decipher a meaning, the words blurring in front of her. Leaning against the counter, she forced herself to breathe and read the paragraph again, mouthing the words, trying to make it more clear.

In the event of the demise of either of the afore-mentioned parties, the surviving party may, at his option, purchase from the heir of the dece-dent, the aforesaid property for its market value as determined by an average of three appraisals.

She glanced up at him. He stared back at her, his face set in stone.

"Did you read it?"

"Yes, but I don't get it." Her heart was racing and her eyes dropped to the page again.

"It means I have the legal right to buy you out and that's what I plan to do. You can talk to a lawyer, but I've checked it out and it's all cut-and-dried."

She glared at him. "Everything is always *cut-and-dried* for you, isn't it?" His eyebrows raised slightly, and she could tell her question rocked him a little. She didn't need an answer—she didn't even know why she'd bothered to ask the question.

She sighed. Exhaustion and a raging headache worked its way into her skull. She'd had enough of J. D. Pruitt and his heart of stone. She was tired of fighting what she couldn't fight anymore. *If I don't fight, then he can't win!*

The thought ripped through her mind and she took another breath.

11

To J.D.'s amazement, she didn't demand an answer to her question. All she did was hand him back the contract, close her eyes and massage her temples.

The dull ache in his stomach haunted him, but he'd done what he wanted to do—protect her. It tore at his gut to see the look of distrust and hurt in her eyes. But it was better this way.

Her lids flashed open, and she pointed a finger at him. "You can have my half of the ranch. I love the Circle C, but I couldn't share it with you. Obviously, from what that document states, I couldn't fight you anyway."

"Good," he forced himself to say. The look one small word brought to her face almost made him double over.

Her anger grew again with a velocity he'd never seen before. "I'll be out of here by tomorrow morning," she snapped.

The thought of her actually leaving and taking Charlie hadn't been fully assimilated. Although he wanted her gone, the reality of it was a brutal picture. "You don't have to hurry," slipped out before he could stop the words.

"*I don't have to hurry?* Believe me, J.D., I can't get out of this hellhole fast enough."

"Hellhole? Just what does that mean?" He narrowed his eyes.

"Do I have to spell it out?" She stared at him, her mouth trembling with anger. "This house, the ranch, mean nothing to me anymore. The place isn't worth it. I'm sure Uncle Charlie wouldn't expect me to be miserable."

She took a breath and pointed at him again. "Then there's you. I actually thought you were a nice guy, and cared for Charlie and me. But with my taste in men, I should have known better. If you think I'm going to stay under the same roof with you for one extra minute, you're dead wrong." She drew her finger back into a clenched fist and shook it at him. "You're a shell of a man. You have no feelings and to compare you to my ex-husband would be a compliment." She laughed unsteadily, dropping her head and shaking it slowly.

"I'm not anything like—"

"Maybe not like him, but you will be. You're a robot without any feelings at all and you like it that way. You think you're lucky to get the ranch all to yourself, well let me clue you in...I wouldn't have a partner like *you*." She choked the last word out. "I feel sorry for you, J.D." She pushed past him and left the kitchen.

The wall clock ticked each second, and he didn't believe what had just happened. He'd done what he'd intended to do, what he'd wanted to do. So why did he feel liked he'd just been hit in the head with a two-by-four?

The ticking kept time with the low pulsing in his head. He glanced around the cold, empty kitchen. It was back to the way it was before Kate and Charlie had come into his life—and so was his heart.

* * *

"You sure you want this job?" Meg asked, then eyed her like she was a fish in a market.

"I want it and I need it. I'll be the best receptionist you've ever had," Kate promised. Standing in the middle of Meg's office, she held Charlie on one hip. This morning she'd packed up most of their belongings and thrown them in her car. After she talked Meg into hiring her, she was planning on renting the furnished bungalow down the street, borrowing a truck from the gas station and getting the rest of her and Charlie's belongings from the Circle C. After that she'd never go back there again.

Meg took Charlie out of her arms and kissed him on the cheek. "I've never had a receptionist, so you don't have any competition for the best. I can't believe how much this kid has grown in the past few weeks." She cradled him in her arm and gave him another kiss. "He's a beautiful baby."

"Thank you. He's why I want to work for you. I'll want to bring Charlie in the office, if that's okay. I can work around his schedule, and he's really good. That's what I did at the ranch, and it worked out all right." The last few words brought a rush of feelings back and she hesitated for a moment. Determined she wouldn't show her emotion, she forced a smile.

"Of course you know I don't mind. I'd love to have him around the office all day. I really need a secretary." She stopped, gazed at Kate, a look of wonder on her face. "But if you're not working on the ranch anymore…why don't you take a job teaching? I know the junior high school can use a good teacher or two—"

"Then I wouldn't be able to spend the day with Charlie. That's important to me. When he goes to school I'll go back to teaching, but that was why I moved out here in the first place. I wanted to be with him.'' She reached out and stroked his arm. He *was* the reason she'd moved to the Circle C. Her purpose didn't need to change just because she'd been naive and misjudged J.D.

Meg gazed at her again with her doctor's stare. ''I don't mean to be nosy, but what happened?''

Kate drew in a breath, knowing the question was coming, and she wasn't exactly sure how to answer it. She didn't want to bad-mouth J.D. He was her cousin, after all. ''It's just not working out between us on the ranch. And the sooner I get settled, the better. J.D. doesn't need a partner.'' The fact floated around the room and came back and hit her square-on.

Meg was silent for a long time, her hand on her chin, her gaze downward. ''He can be awfully stubborn. I thought maybe you two might hit it off. You're both quite a bit alike—''

''We are nothing alike!'' Her hand cut through the air and Charlie jumped at the harsh tone. Kate brought her voice back to normal. ''Sorry, but it just won't work. I want to go on with my life. The quicker I forget about the Circle C, the better.''

Meg forced her lips into a semi-grin. ''Well, I hate to work off J.D.'s bad luck for losing you, but sure, come to work for me. My office is a mess of paperwork, insurance claims and dirty coffee cups. I can't pay you a lot, but if it works out, I'll give you a raise in a month.'' Meg brought Charlie's fat cheek to her lips again and gave him another kiss. ''Welcome aboard, little guy.''

''You look lousy.'' A warm autumn-like breeze fanned at Meg's hair, and the early morning sun shined down on her concerned face.

"Thank you, Doctor Meg," J.D. said, not bothering to hide the sarcasm in his voice. "Just the kind of diagnosis I like." He'd been working in the pens when his cousin dropped by unexpectedly.

"It's not a diagnosis. You wouldn't want to hear that either. It's only an observation. But the way you look, I'd recommend you come in for a checkup. You've lost weight, and the circles around your eyes could be used for bull's eyes." She scanned him from head to toe. "To put it bluntly, cousin, you look like death warmed over."

J.D. nodded his head once. "Yeah, well, I've had better days." His own words stung but they were true. He still wasn't sleeping, and food tasted like boiled cardboard. Determined, he was fighting his feelings all the way—for Kate and Charlie's sake.

Shoving her hands in her jean's pockets, Meg leaned against the chain-link fence. "Is that the ostrich that kicked Kate?"

"Nah, that renegade is long gone. Those two are about gone too. Tomorrow I'm having another rancher pick them up. That's Herman and Jezabel." He stared at the two birds.

"Herman and Jezabel? That sounds like a little of Kate's influence."

J.D. let his mouth curl into a grin. "Yeah, I told her not to name them and not to get attached but she didn't listen."

"Why are you getting rid of them?"

"Cause they won't do what comes naturally. I'm into breeding these birds, not keeping them for pets. Those two," he nodded to them again, "have had enough time to get acquainted and do the deed."

Meg raised her left brow and laughed. "Sounds like some humans I know. By the way, I've hired a secretary."

"'Bout time. Now when I call I won't get your machine?"

Meg nodded. "Correct. She works nine to five and she's good."

"Who'd you hire?" J.D. stood his legs akimbo, arms crossed eyeing her curiously.

"Kate."

Just hearing her name made his stomach tighten.

"The woman is organized. I told her when she first started I couldn't pay her a lot, but she didn't seem to mind. Her main focus was bringing Charlie to work with her. They brighten up the office like you wouldn't believe." Meg gazed at him, her eyes narrowing.

"I know how they can brighten a place up," he said quietly. The starkness of his own statement sent a jolt to his gut. He thought he'd start to forget her sooner. Although stunned, he was glad to know she and Charlie were safe and settled.

A smile crept over Meg's face. "If you're interested, she reacts the same way when I mention your name, but she's ignoring that fact too. She's got more bags under her eyes than you do. What the hell did the two of you do to each other?"

Meg's directness didn't surprise him. After twenty-eight years he expected nothing less from her. "Not a thing. Just wanted the ranch back...the way it was before. It's better for both of them to be out of here." Only the last words he believed.

"How's it good for them? They were happy until you lost it. What's wrong with you?" Her eyebrows shot up, and she waited for an answer. The silence between them was broken by Herman's booming. When he didn't answer her, she continued. "J.D. you can't go on living your life so isolated. Nobody likes being alone. You had a good chance with Kate."

He liked being alone—always had. Quickly he mentally declared his last thought a lie. He'd talked himself into being a loner. When Ann was alive, he'd loved her company, and then when Kate and Charlie had come along he'd felt happy again.

His cousin continued. "She was perfect for you."

"Yeah, she was perfect for me, but I'm not perfect for her. Just like Ann...." He stopped himself before speaking the rest of his thoughts. Rehashing what he'd done to Ann was time wasted.

"What kind of logic are you using?" Meg took her hands out of her pockets and pressed them against her hips. "'Just like Ann!' What the hell does that mean?" There was another long silence between them. She turned to look at the birds and chewed on her bottom lip.

Turning half around, she stared at him for a long moment, her eyes growing wet. "You know James Dean, I loved Ann too and I miss her, but life has to go on. I could have taken the blame just as easily as you did." She brought her hand up and pointed a finger at his chest. "You weren't the only one that was hurt. But Ann wouldn't have wanted either of us to be the way you are. You know that as well as I do." She brought her hand back to her waist.

He didn't answer her. His reasoning had been in place for so long, it was almost impossible to believe anything else. No, Ann wouldn't want him to blame himself, but he couldn't help it.

"Grow up, cousin. You've got to take the good with the bad in life and start living your life." She took his hand. "Don't take the easy way out. You didn't kill Ann. It was an accident—it had nothing to do with you or me, it was just *fate*. You're not responsible." She stared at him, a pleading look growing stronger.

There was no answer for her.

"I've got to get to the office, J.D. I don't mean to intrude, but that's never stopped me before." She paused and tried to smile but couldn't. "Grow up. There's no boogie man out there waiting to get anyone you decide to care about."

Her statement startled him. "You'd better go to work. You're talking crazy."

J.D. sat behind Kate's small desk in the hatching barn. It looked exactly as she'd left it—pencils and pens in a neat holder, notepad in the right corner and calendar turned to correct day and month with chores noted.

He let his breath out in a whoosh. Anxious energy pushed him out of the chair, and he walked to the incubator. The full shelves rotated slowly in the same pattern they always had. Checking the temperature, he found it was fine, but the humidity was a little low. J.D. tapped the dial, checked it again, then turned the regulator knob. The moisture level would be up to normal in a few minutes. They hadn't had any more problems with the incubator.

Turning, he caught a glimpse of his reflection in the plate-glass viewing window. Not too many weeks ago Kate stood next to him in the same spot. They'd both been so excited when the incubator finally kicked on and they could go back up to the house.

His breath caught in his chest again, and he blocked the thoughts. That part of his life was over now. The memories would be back, no matter what, but he'd deal with them. It would take time—just like it had with Ann.

Back at the desk he pulled open a drawer in hopes of finding a file he needed. The inside of the drawer was like the rest of the barn, neat and clean. Kate had organized everything and filed all the orders. When her uncle used the desk it was always a mess.

Finding the folder he needed, he thumbed through it. The facts and figures were all there. He studied Kate's script. It was without unnecessary flourishes, yet feminine and soft, and reminded him of her so much his throat hurt when he stared at it.

His gaze traveled around the small area. Charlie's stroller and playpen were gone. He missed the little guy more than he thought he would. The ranch was empty now.

He turned back to the desk and his paperwork. Kate handled the daily tallies and the correspondence and he'd almost forgotten how it was done. He needed the address of a buyer who called this morning and wanted information on the hatchlings. He rummaged through each drawer again.

His eyes ached from lack of sleep. Dreams of laughing and kissing and talking with Kate surrounded him at night and left him depressed when he woke up. He dreamed of their lovemaking, of Kate's tender caress and her sweet lips against his own. Her gently heaving breath lifting her up to him. Their need for each other weaving out of control—wild tenderness melting into concentrated cravings which left him awake and hot with desire.

But nightmares haunted him, too, and reminded him. Gut-wrenching dreams of Charlie crying and Kate groaning with pain that made him sit straight up in bed and wipe the sweat off his face, trying to catch his breath. Those dreams seared his mind and kept him up for the rest of the night—and kept him from finding her and Charlie and bringing them back to the ranch.

Pushing himself back from the desk, he pulled out the top desk drawer with such a fury, it came off the track and into his hands. With the sudden move he tried to right the drawer and in doing so tipped the contents out. A heavy metal stapler fell on his booted toe.

"Son of a—" J.D. yelled, and his voice echoed through the barn. He dropped the drawer to the floor and the dry, antiquated wood shattered. Another more profound string of expletives echoed through the barn. Now he'd have to put the drawer back together, as if he didn't have enough to do.

He stood, pushed the chair to the back wall and knelt down by the pieces. Each joint had broken, and there was a large crack in the bottom of the drawer. J.D. picked up two pieces and put them together.

As he was about to stand, a slash of white caught his eye. A piece of paper had fallen and wedged itself in the side of the drawer. Maybe it was the address he needed. J.D. put the pieces of the drawer down, reached up and picked the paper out of the crack behind the drawer. It was an envelope. Sitting on the cement floor, he leaned his back against the desk. The scrawly script on the front of the envelope belonged to Uncle Charlie. It was only partially addressed and almost unreadable.

J.D. stared at it, trying to make out the name or address, then turned the envelope over in his hands, his mind roiling with thoughts about his old partner.

He and Charlie had a mutual respect between them. He was a good friend—like the father he never had.

He hated to throw the letter out. If Charlie had written it, then it was important that it get mailed. Turning it over again, J.D. studied the illegible name. Maybe there was an address inside. He worked the flap of the envelope open and pulled the paper out and unfolded it. The handwriting was much clearer, but there was no address at the top. J.D. started to fold the letter into thirds when he hesitated—a legible word catching his eye.

Regret!

Hell, he didn't think Charlie regretted anything. When he was around the ranch, he was happy-go-lucky. J.D. unfolded the letter again. He didn't want to be a snoop, but maybe there was a clue in the body of the letter about who to send it to.

Holding the paper in one hand, he let his eyes scan the first two lines.

My Darling Carrie,
There is one moment I regret in my life...

J.D. stopped reading and scratched his head with his free hand. He didn't even know Charlie had a girlfriend. A chuckle came to his lips. The old fox kept that part of his life a secret. Never mentioned a woman and never seemed to be interested in having a relationship, always saying he was too old, and it was hard to teach old dogs new tricks.

Out of curiosity, J.D.'s eyes scanned back to the letter.

For one brief moment I gave up on our love because of hurt and pain. Afraid to love you, silly as it might sound. Yes, love scared me. But now that my life is almost over, I realize how silly and foolish I was. If I have one sorrow, it will always be that I didn't trust fate. You can never forgive me, and I understand, my darling Carrie. I only have myself to blame.

He stopped reading and fought Charlie's words. They were like a vise around his heart. Slowly he folded the letter and opened the envelope. A newspaper clipping he hadn't seen before floated to the floor. J.D. put the letter and envelope down and picked the clipping up. It was the woman's obituary. His partner never had a chance to send the letter.

He couldn't think about all this now. The meaning of Charlie's words he'd just read pulsed and grew and reverberated around the barn as if his old partner was standing next to him reading the letter out loud, telling him he was a fool, too.

At one time Charlie's laughter poured throughout the ranch—but it hid his deep loss and pain.

Shoving the letter in a side drawer and slamming it shut, more expletives flew around the room. Why in the hell did he have to find the letter and read the damned thing? He'd already run Kate off the ranch just like he wanted. He rubbed his forehead with the pads of his fingers. A nightmarish thought grabbed at his mind and ripped at his soul.

Would he be like Charlie—writing to Kate when it was too late?

12

A few days later, J.D. stood alone outside the pen. He inhaled and let his gaze travel around the Circle C. It was a typical September day in Texas. He'd seen plenty of them. When hot summer days waned and a slight crispness filled the air. He remembered Kate saying she was looking forward to fall. He would miss the special time with her. The bonfires, walking at night when the air was thick with burning autumn leaves, the homecoming football game at the high school and Halloween.

The visions of the three of them together roved through his mind and sent a smile to his face. What would Charlie look like all dressed up in a Halloween costume? He'd miss that, too. The thought caused a strangeness to circle his heart. A white-hot dullness traveled through him, jolting him into the reality of what his so-called life had become.

Out of sheer desperation to get his mind off the turmoil, he returned to collecting eggs. He needed to get Herman and Jezabel ready for the transfer.

He walked across the pen to check their water and feed. Herman strutted back and forth across the dirt and craned his neck at him. "Too late, buddy. You blew it. You should have started your courting of that little lady months ago," J.D. yelled at the bird, but his attention was quickly drawn away by the egg lying in the nest. He doubted if it were fertile. Yet, somehow, hope crawled through his mind. He should check one more time.

His gaze traveled back to the pair. Herman boomed and Jezabel fluffed her feathers, squatted, waiting for her partner. J.D. hooked his thumbs into his back pockets and stared. He wouldn't have believed the sight if he hadn't seen it with his own eyes. Turning back to the egg, he picked it up gently. He rolled the still-warm shell in his hands and then cradled it in his arm as he walked back to the hatching barn.

In the darkened room he held the light up to it.

"Damn."

J.D. walked with the egg in his hands back to their pen. He glanced at the birds and smiled. Jezabel was fluttering her feathers again, and Herman, on a dead run, headed toward her. J.D.'s mind drifted back to the day little Charlie was born. His birth had been a miracle. The reality of it all was too much to deny.

Maybe miracles were possible.

That evening as J.D. sat on the couch, he thought about Kate. He'd read Charlie's letter again, and together with Meg's words, different thoughts flourished in his mind.

Grow up cousin, there's no bogey man! Meg always had an uncanny way of cutting to the chase when it came to knowing what was going on inside his head.

He'd brought Herman's and Jezabel's egg into the house, and he gazed at it. He and Kate had laughed at how she'd gotten so attached to the birds. One day he'd taken her hands in his own and advised her not to look at the animals like pets, but she'd laughed at him and told him she couldn't help it. After, she'd asked him to give Jezabel and Herman another chance, another month to get to know each other; he had agreed.

Her advice proved right. Instead of selling the birds for next to nothing, he had two mating birds that would probably produce hundreds of eggs.

Kate was right about a lot of things.

Kate glanced at Charlie, who slept soundly in the playpen in the corner. She sighed and turned back to the diminishing paperwork that covered her desk. It had been a week since she'd moved from the Circle C, and she was pretty much situated in the small house she'd rented. Working for Meg was satisfying. Everything in her life should be okay, but it wasn't.

Her anger had subsided, and she was able to think about what happened without fury choking her. Sometimes late at night when Charlie was sound asleep and she lay in bed, her thoughts tumbled down to a place where she held all her memories. She tried to figure out what had gone wrong between J.D. and herself.

And late at night when she thought of him, she remembered the look in his eyes when he'd told her to leave the ranch. Being away from the situation, where her heart and her feelings weren't twisted and tumbled by outrage, she knew J.D. had reacted out of pain. She didn't know why, but something inside told her not to be angry at him.

Twisting her mouth into a pout and turning back to the desk, she started the last of her paperwork. J.D. had to heal his own heart if he could. She couldn't do it for him. But he'd been so badly wounded she wasn't sure that was possible. It was one thing he had to do alone—one thing a partner couldn't help with.

She sighed. There would never be another J.D. in her life. Maybe someday he'd meet someone he could love. The thought caused a sharp pain to form in her chest, and her mind filled with memories of their times together.

"I'm taking my lunch break," Meg announced, peeking her head around the corner.

"Going to the Sunshine?" Kate asked as her boss came out to the reception area.

Meg turned and smiled. "Yes. I'll bring you back a sandwich if you'd like. It's nice to be able to take a lunch hour. How's the billing going?"

"Fine. You had it all together. I just put it in order. All the bills should be in the mail by tomorrow."

"My patients will love it. Haven't received a bill from me in months." Meg pulled her purse over her shoulder and grinned again. She studied her wristwatch. "I'd better get going. What time's my first afternoon appointment?"

"Not till one-thirty."

The door opened suddenly, and J.D. stood in the light with an ostrich egg cradled in his left arm and a worried look on his face. Stepping inside the office, he waited for the door to shut before he took his right hand off the bar.

The three of them stared at one another, no one saying a word.

"Sorry, James Dean, I don't do ostriches. The vet's right down the street," Meg announced, and then chuckled. "What are you bringing that egg in here for?"

Kate swallowed hard and placed her fingertips against the desk, gripping it tightly. She didn't need any more confrontations with him. Demanding that her heart stop beating so fast, she pressed her lips together.

"Didn't bring the egg in for you. Brought it to Kate." He nodded toward her, his steely gaze riveted.

Meg looked at him, her mouth half open, then she turned to Kate and back to J.D. "If I don't leave now, I won't have a lunch hour. Have a nice chat." Before anyone could say another word, Meg stepped around J.D. and was out the door.

He was still staring at her, but Kate couldn't even say his name out loud she was so afraid her voice would break, or it wouldn't be there at all. Even though it had only been a week since she'd seen him, it felt like years. The undisguised look of pain in his brown eyes hit her with a sheer force of a punch, and she forgot any leftover pain or anger he'd made her feel.

"I've been an idiot and a stupid jerk," he said, the words coming out fast.

"Yes, you have." Her statement was just as blunt, and for a moment she didn't care if she hurt him. But her words made the corners of his mouth turn up.

"Glad you agree with me." He was still staring into her eyes, the seriousness of his gaze gripping her heart and softening it. "I'm tired of playing it safe. Wouldn't blame you if you didn't forgive me, and I'll understand, but I'll never give up trying to prove to you that I love you."

She felt her eyes start to tear at the words, and she turned her head away from him. She heard his footsteps as he moved toward her. His fingers wrapped around her upper arm, and he gently pulled her from behind the desk.

"I swear to God that I won't try to tell you what to do. I won't run your life. We'll make all the decisions together at the ranch. You, me and Charlie." His chest expanded after he said the last word and waited for her to respond.

Kate blinked, hoping she wasn't dreaming, a little bit of her wishing she was. "What are you trying to say?"

He closed his eyes and inhaled deeply, then opened them and stared intently into hers again. "I'm saying that I want you and Charlie to come back to the Circle C. I want us to be a family. That's where you both belong. I made a big mistake when Ann died. Blamed her accident on myself. Time I stop." His fingers massaged her arm, and the warmth she felt from him was real. "Kate, marry me."

The silence between them was only interrupted by Charlie's sleepy breathing. "J.D., I'm not sure."

His finger went to her lips and he caressed her mouth. "Kate, Charlie needs a daddy, and we need each other. Can't promise you I'll be a perfect husband, but I'll try damned hard." He searched her face. "I found a letter that your uncle Charlie wrote to a woman." He hesitated and drew in a breath. "He made a mistake, like I did. But I'm luckier. I can change things. It's too late for Charlie, don't let it be too late for us."

His gaze pleaded honestly with her. "I love you, Kate, and I don't want to lose you."

She loved him, too. He stood in front of her holding an ostrich egg, telling her that he wanted to marry her and be a daddy to Charlie. Her heart beat faster with love and the sincere promises he'd just made.

"Why did you bring the egg in?" She let herself smile the way she wanted to. She dropped her gaze down to the egg, then glanced up. The deadly hurt was gone. The harmful secrets he'd been hiding behind had been torn away.

He held the egg in front of her with both hands. "*This* is Herman and Jezabel's fertile egg. I checked it. When I candled it, I knew it was a miracle." He rolled the egg in his hands and she stared at it in wonder.

"Looks like we'll have to rename Herman, he isn't a confirmed bachelor," she announced, and smiled.

He placed the egg gingerly on her desk and stepped closer to her. "If that dumb rooster can see the light, I guess I can, too. What do you think, Kate? Will you come back to the ranch and be my wife and let me help you take care of Charlie?"

She wrapped her arms around him, not saying a word. She wanted to enjoy every moment. To feel the very warmth of him. They'd work together to make a life for themselves and Charlie. They'd grow and learn together. She leaned back and looked up into his eyes. "I think Charlie would like that very much. He misses you."

"And what about his mother?" he asked calmly, seriously.

"I love you, and yes, I'll marry you...as long as we can be partners, too. Fifty-fifty."

J.D. pulled her closer to him and wrapped his arms tight around her, his mouth searching for hers and finding it. They exchanged a loving kiss and then he pulled back, a grin covering his face. Tracing the outline of her lips with his index finger, he spoke. "We'll be good together, Kate. We'll be the best partners in the entire county…heck, in the entire State of Texas.''

Kate touched her lips to his once more. Anything was possible with J.D.

* * * * *

Take 4 bestselling love stories FREE

Plus get a FREE surprise gift!

Special Limited-time Offer

Mail to Silhouette Reader Service™

> **3010 Walden Avenue**
> **P.O. Box 1867**
> **Buffalo, N.Y. 14269-1867**

YES! Please send me 4 free Silhouette Yours Truly™ novels and my free surprise gift. Then send me 4 brand-new novels every other month, which I will receive months before they appear in bookstores. Bill me at the low price of $2.90 each plus 25¢ delivery and applicable sales tax, if any.* That's the complete price and a savings of over 10% off the cover prices—quite a bargain! I understand that accepting the books and gift places me under no obligation ever to buy any books. I can always return a shipment and cancel at any time. Even if I never buy another book from Silhouette, the 4 free books and the surprise gift are mine to keep forever.

201 SEN CF2X

Name	(PLEASE PRINT)

Address	Apt. No.

City	State	Zip

This offer is limited to one order per household and not valid to present Silhouette Yours Truly™ subscribers. *Terms and prices are subject to change without notice. Sales tax applicable in N.Y.

USYRT-296

©1996 Harlequin Enterprises Limited

PAULA DETMER RIGGS

**Continues the
twelve-book series—
36 Hours—in May 1998
with Book Eleven**

THE PARENT PLAN

Cassidy and Karen Sloane's marriage was on the rocks—and had been since their little girl spent one lonely, stormy night trapped in a cave. And it would take their daughter's wisdom and love to convince the stubborn rancher and the proud doctor that they had better things to do than clash over their careers, because their most important job was being Mom and Dad—and husband and wife.

For Cassidy and Karen and *all* the residents of Grand Springs, Colorado, the storm-induced blackout was just the beginning of 36 Hours that changed *everything!* You won't want to miss a single book.

Available at your favorite retail outlet.